Etched Upon the Heart

IN THE SPIRIT OF LOVE

KATHRYN KALEIGH

IN THE SPIRIT OF LOVE

(Reading Order)

Spirits of the Heart

Out of Dreams and Ashes

Etched Upon the Heart

ETCHED UPON THE HEART

PREVIEW — ACCIDENTALLY FOREVER

Copyright © 2024 by Kathryn Kaleigh

Written by Kathryn Kaleigh.

Published by Kathryn Kaleigh Books 2024

Cover by Skyhouse24Media

www.kathrynkaleigh.com

Etched Upon the Heart

Chapter One

Amanda Gray

Tonight was going to be a rowdy night.

It was spring and there was a new crew of men in from Denver. Carpenters mostly.

Whiskey Springs was booming. New houses were going up. New businesses.

A church. A school. Even a new sheriff's office.

From the time I woke in the mornings until right before the sun started to set, I heard what I thought of as dueling hammers.

The crosscut saws didn't make so much noise, but the hammers filled the air with a never-ending off-key chorus.

It was noticeable mostly because it was in stark contrast to the quietness of winter. In winter, no one built anything. Winter was a time of survival.

Even the saloon was quiet in the winter. A few regulars who lived in town coming in for a drink and a game of cards. Some conversation. Trappers coming through now and then, bringing in their stacks of furs, taking a break from the harsh mountain life.

Through the window in the saloon, I could see the rugged mountain peaks that surrounded the valley, still covered in snow.

The snow wasn't done with us, but it would be light now. Mother Nature went easy on us in the month of May.

Flowers bloomed. Trees bloomed. Outdoors smelled fresh like a pine forest and the brisk wind-swept hints of that freshness indoors.

The sun's warmth melted away most of the snow, leaving patches of snow beneath the spruce trees to remind us of the winter we had survived.

I didn't mind. I didn't mind any of it.

I stood behind the bar of the Whiskey Springs Saloon and scanned the room.

Molly was on piano tonight. She was quite good and her music was lively and uplifting. Sometimes I envied Molly. She was allowed to dress in a completely different style than I was.

Tonight Molly wore a red dress with a white underskirt. The dress was shorter in front than in the back and came almost all the way up to her knees in the front. It was low-cut at the bodice and sleeveless. It was the kind of dress showgirls wore. Not that Molly was a showgirl, but it was her job to attract customers.

Papa would never let me wear a dress like that. Even when I played the piano, he wouldn't let me wear anything like the dresses Molly and the other girl who played piano got to wear.

The dress I was currently wearing was pale emerald green, a

pretty color I'd picked out myself. It had long narrow sleeves and a high, demure neckline. A million buttons down the front.

It was part of the agreement Papa and I had made years ago. I remembered it well. I had been twelve years old and Mama had just gone back east to take care of her mother. Papa couldn't leave me home by myself, so he'd brought me to the saloon with him. Since Papa owned the saloon, no one thought anything about a child being there.

It hadn't taken me long to get bored, so I'd started learning. I'd learned about the different drinks and since I already knew how to count money, I was practically running the bar by the time I was thirteen.

Mama had left seven years ago. She was still in Savannah taking care of her mother. I read the letters that she and Papa wrote each other. Sometimes they talked about Mama bringing Grandma—a woman I had never even met—out here with her, but apparently Grandma wasn't well enough to travel for the three plus months it would take for her to get from Savannah, Georgia to Whiskey Springs, Colorado.

Sometimes they talked about me going to live with Mama, but Papa wasn't willing to let me travel alone and he couldn't leave the saloon that long to take me.

I didn't want to leave Whiskey Springs. Whiskey Springs was my home and the saloon was my world.

I was nineteen now.

I worked alongside Papa in the saloon every night. The customers knew me. They knew my father owned the saloon and they were all respectful and yet Papa never left me alone for more than a few minutes.

We lived in a little cabin behind the saloon. Sometimes he would leave me at home alone, but I could tell he didn't like it. He always made me lock the door in the evenings.

It didn't seem necessary. Whiskey Springs was a peaceful town and my uncle was the sheriff.

But Papa and me, we did just fine.

I guess he worried because I was what he called "of age."

I'd had six marriage proposals that I knew of. There were others Papa didn't tell me about. I'd bet money on it.

It didn't matter to me that I was "of age." I had no interest in getting married. Getting married would mean leaving the saloon.

Even now Papa was teaching me how to keep the books.

He'd told me several times over that one day the saloon would be mine.

"Pumpkin," Papa said. He called me Pumpkin when there was no one else listening.

I reached high to pull a bottle of whiskey from one of the shelves behind the bar.

"Yes, Papa?" I took the bottle of whiskey, opened it, and set it down beneath the bar. We'd be needing it soon.

"I think it's time you took a husband."

Chapter Two

Shawn Richard
1870

The trip had been a disaster from the get go. The first disaster was when my cow's milk dried up. Not a good start to a three-month long trek across the prairie.

Fortunately, my neighbors were generous and they knew as well as I did that when it came time to turn Erma into nourishment, I would share with them.

I would be putting that off, though. Erma had

been my cow since before the war and she was
more like a pet than a main dish.
    I didn't tell anyone that, though, of course.
That wasn't the kind of thing a man was supposed
to admit to.

I SAT BACK in my chair and reread the words I had just written.

I sat in an upstairs room in a boarding house. Typical for a small town in the wild west. It was either this or the saloon. At least here I didn't have to think so much about what typically went on in the bed.

The room had the basics. A little bed that slept well enough and the sheets smelled freshly laundered.

Besides, the bed, there a little dresser with a water pitcher and basin. A lantern. A couple of candles. That was just about it.

My trunk, sitting at the end of the bed, served as a chair.

From the sound of things going on outside the open window —men yelling, wagons rolling past—it was going to be a rowdy night. I'd heard the little town was rough, but rumors were just that. Rumors. Sometimes they were right. Sometimes not. Looked liked the rumors, in this case, had been right.

Writing the first few pages of a new book was always the hardest part.

That meant that Mondays were the hardest part of my work day.

Started a new book on Monday. Finished that book on Friday. Wrapped it up and mailed it off on Saturday.

Week after week after week.

Some weeks I moved around on Saturday and Sunday, scoping out where I wanted to spend my week. Sometimes I stayed in the same little town for weeks at the time. Especially in winter. I stayed in the same little town for three months last winter.

But it was spring now and my feet were itchy to move along.

I had what my sister called the wanderlust.

Didn't want to stay in one place for very long.

My writing schedule, though, had me staying put in a place for a week at the time. It was how I maintained my prolific writing schedule.

This little room I'd booked through Saturday had everything I needed and more. I was a man of few needs.

I had a bed with a soft mattress. A dresser with a pitcher of fresh water sitting in a wash basin.

And most of all, I had a writing desk. A writing desk was a prerequisite to any place I rented.

If the room didn't come with a writing desk, I'd throw some money around and one would show up. The little towns didn't always have reams of paper, though, so I stayed ahead on that. Paper, an ink well, and pens. Tools of my trade.

A dime novel writer.

I'd grown up reading them and somewhere along the way, I'd started writing them. I'd started writing them in secret first, not even telling my older sister, Olivia.

Olivia and I had been close. She and I had traveled across the prairie ourselves. That was five years ago. She was married now. Living in a cabin out in the middle of nowhere.

I'd written dozens of books in that cabin. It was a nice, peaceful place and I always had a room there. But, as Olivia said, I had the wanderlust.

I needed coffee. That's what I needed.

Maybe I'd find some inspiration for my next cast of characters. That was another of the reasons I liked to move around so much.

I created brand new characters every Monday, so being in a new town with new people was helpful in that particular area.

People never knew that I was using them as characters in my novels. I was good at mixing it up so they never knew.

That was half the fun of writing, for me at least. Making up people and situations.

I went downstairs and out the front door of the boarding house owned by a little old lady whose husband had passed away just last year.

Her name was Lucy and I'd already made her into one of my characters on the wagon train. Her new name in my book was Mary. My characters didn't need fancy names to be entertaining.

I walked down Main Street of the little town called Independence and found a diner. They had decent coffee and while I was there, I had a slice of apple pie.

I took out a pencil and made a few notes about people I could use in future stories. I had notebooks full of them. Each time I used one of them, I marked through them. It was a pretty good system. Not that anyone would notice if I repeated a character.

I distinctly remembered devouring hundreds of paperback

stories when I was a boy. I never noticed details like that. Or maybe it wasn't so much that I didn't notice as it was I didn't care.

I loved diving into a new story and I'd stay with it until I finished it. Typically took me no more than a few hours to plow through one of them.

After finishing up my coffee and pie, I wandered down to the General Store. Maybe they had a ream of paper so I could restock my supply.

This particular town was in the valley. Wasn't sure how I ended up here.

I already missed the mountains. Saturday I would pack up and head back to the hills.

Getting to move around was probably one of my biggest motivators to finish a book. Unless, of course, I liked the town. Still. I liked having the option of moving around.

That and the regular checks my publisher deposited in my account. I was one of the most consistent writers my publisher had. Or so he said. I'd written a book every week for the last three years.

It had taken me a little time to get my momentum going, but once I did, I stayed with it.

The General Store had just about anything a man could want. Candles. Flour. Axes. Bolts of material.

Personally, I didn't need any of those things. I never cooked. I never cut my own firewood. And I had a tailor in Denver who made my clothes for me.

I was checking out a shelf of hats, thinking about buying a new one, when a flyer pinned to the wall caught my attention.

It was an advertisement for an opera. But it wasn't the opera that caught my attention. I could take or leave opera. It was the location that caught my attention.

Whiskey Springs.

I had another sister, Ember, who lived near Whiskey Springs, but I'd never done more than ride through the little town itself.

Maybe it was time to do more than just ride through Whiskey Springs.

Whiskey Springs sounded like a good name for a town in my next few books. I could do a series.

In the meantime, I had some work to do on the book I'd just started.

Chapter Three

AMANDA

Still holding an empty glass in my hand, I turned and looked at my father.

He had lost his sanity. I'd heard of that kind of thing happening.

There was a place back east called an insane asylum where they put people who lost their sanity.

Just a couple of weeks ago, a wagon had come through with three women locked inside. Apparently they had all lost their sanity for a variety of reasons.

Papa had explained to me that the wild, unstructured west did that to people sometimes. It was more than they could handle.

For some reason, I had gotten the impression that it was mostly women who lost their sanity.

"Do you need to sit down, Papa?"

I pulled over a wooden stool and guided him to sit.

Not sure what to do with the empty glass in my hand, I decided to pour some of that whiskey I'd just opened into it.

I pressed the glass into my father's hands.

"You should drink this," I said. "It'll make you feel better."

"I don't need a whiskey, Pumpkin," Papa said, setting the glass on the counter.

"I'm worried about you, Papa." I walked from one side of him to the other. "I don't want them to come and take you away. I don't want them to put you in the insane asylum."

Papa laughed.

"It's not funny, Papa," I said, putting my hands on my hips. "It's not funny for you to go and scare me like this."

"I'm not insane. I've just been thinking."

Gaping at him in disbelief, I dragged our other stool over and sat down next to him.

We had half a dozen men in the saloon right now, but they were all focused on a game of cards, not paying us any mind.

Good. I needed to sort this thing out with Papa before the saloon filled up for the evening.

"You know I'm not going to get married. I'm going to stay here and run the saloon."

"Your mother and I have been talking."

"Did you get a letter from her? Did the postman bring a letter yesterday?"

If he had, Papa hadn't shown me. He almost always shared Mama's letters with me. It was our only way of keeping in touch with her.

"Yes," he said. "She agrees. You're too old to be working in this saloon without a husband."

"Nonsense," I said, standing up again and going back to wiping down glasses. "You should drink your whiskey."

"You know I don't drink," he said absently. "This is a serious matter."

"And who would you have me marry?" I made a wild gesture toward the men playing cards. "The old widower Mr. Jones? Or the blacksmith Mr... what's his name?"

"Wyatt."

"Yes. Mr. Wyatt." I whirled back on my father. "Why, Papa?"

"Never mind," he said. "We'll talk about it later."

"Good idea. Let's talk about it later." Like never.

When I got home tonight I'd pen a letter to Mama. I'd tell her that Papa's sanity was slipping. Maybe she should try to find a way to get back out here. I know she had her mother to take care of, but Papa needed her, too.

If I let her know just how serious Papa's condition was, she would find a way to get her.

"Actually," Papa said. "I was against it. It was your mother's idea."

Chapter Four

SHAWN

I finished up my book a day early, packed up, and left Independence. It was too rowdy for my blood and that was saying something.

I didn't mind a little rowdy. I used everything I could experience and everything I witnessed in my books. Maybe not right away. But eventually.

But a man had been killed on the street two nights ago. Killed in cold blood.

The fellow hadn't been doing anything wrong. They said he looked at someone wrong.

It could have been me. Sometimes I was so wrapped up in my made up characters that I forgot to pay attention to the real people around me.

It was a good thing I finished my book early. It took me two days to get to Whiskey Springs.

The little town was booming. Buildings going up everywhere. I rode past what must have been a dozen buildings in various stages of going up. Sawing. Hammering. Men moving about everywhere. If I didn't have a job. This would be the place to find work.

The little town had a positive vibe and I could already see my next story forming up in my head.

I spent several hours riding around, looking around for a boarding house where I could lodge for a few days, maybe longer. Finally stopped at the General Store and asked. No boarding houses in Whiskey Springs.

That left the saloon. It had been awhile since I'd stayed in a saloon and the Whiskey Springs Saloon looked like one of the best ones I'd seen.

After I dropped my horse off at the livery, I walked across the street to the saloon. I heard the inviting music before I even reached the doors.

It was nice and clean with a large window that looked out toward the mountain peaks.

The piano music was inviting as I went in through the swinging doors.

There was a card game going on in one corner of the room.

I'd played cards once just for the experience. Once was enough. It wasn't my thing and yet that experience gave me what I needed to write card games into my books.

There was a grizzled fellow sitting on one of the wooden stools.

A young lady in a ruffled red dress sat playing the piano. Her eyes were closed and she didn't seemed to be concerned with anything other than the feel of the keys beneath her fingers.

That was it. There was no one else in the saloon.

Since I didn't see a bartender, I took a seat at the other end of the bar to wait. The wooden bar stool was basic, a little rugged, but sturdy.

The bar itself was a well-rubbed mahogany. I'd say it had seen a lot of activity in its day.

It was over ten years old, if I had to venture a guess. Looked pretty much like every other saloon except for the big window in the front.

Stairs leading up to the second floor where, with any luck, I'd secure a room. I'd start with one week. See how it went.

With nothing to do but wait, I pulled a leather notebook and pencil out of my haversack. While I waited, I could at least take some notes. Figure out the name of the characters for my next book.

Amanda, I decided for the female character.

"Can I get you something, Sir?" It was the beautiful voice of an angel. Just a hint of a southern accent. Just enough that I knew she would be pretty before I even looked up.

"Just some water," I said as I looked up.

The girl not only had the voice of an angel, she had the face of an angel. She was young. Clear, smooth skin that told me she didn't go outside much. Long brunette hair secured on one side.

Full red bow-shaped lips that smiled at me. And those eyes. Green eyes the color of a verdant forest after a rain shower.

"Of course," she said, her eyes lingering on mine a moment

longer than necessary before she turned away to pour a glass of water.

She wore a demure emerald green dress in clear contrast the scanty red dress the piano player wore. This girl was a lady. There was no question about that.

A lady working in a saloon behind the bar.

Intriguing.

She set the glass of water down in front of me. "Anything else?"

"No," I said automatically. Then "Yes. A room if you have one."

"We do. I'll get my father."

So the angel's father worked here, too. The pieces of the puzzle were starting to fall into place.

I added to my notes. *Emerald green gown. Long brunette hair. Green eyes that could lure a sailor onto the dangerous rocks to his demise.*

"You need a room?" A man, appearing in front of me, asked. The man was middle-aged, healthy looking. Pleasant enough, but a no nonsense kind of guy. He wore a neatly trimmed beard and had blue eyes that seemed to size me up in a glance.

"Yes, Sir," I said, closing my notebook. "For the week if you have it."

"You just passing through?" the man asked, glancing at my glass of water.

"Not quite sure yet. My sister lives nearby." Was I being interviewed before I could be given a room?

The man gave me a little nod. Must have been the statement about my sister.

"We have one. I'll get your key."

Maybe the little town was quiet for good reason. Maybe they screened out some of the riff raff before they allowed them in. Having a sister nearby could definitely be to my advantage.

A couple of minutes later, he came back with a big iron key.

"Room's on the end. Best view in the house."

"Thank you. I appreciate that."

"Supper is at six o'clock. Included in the rate."

"Much obliged."

"If you need anything else, just let Amanda know. She'll point you in the right direction."

"I will be needing a de—" Amanda? "Did you say Amanda?"

"My daughter," he said, inclining his head back with a quick gesture.

"I will," I said. "Thank you, Sir."

Left alone again, I sipped my water, then opened my journal again.

It was just a coincidence that I had decided to name my character Amanda, the same name as the beautiful girl working behind the bar.

Maybe I'd heard someone say her name. Whichever it was, it was one hell of a coincidence.

Chapter Five

AMANDA

After I served the new customer a glass of water, Papa sent me to his office to add up some figures in his ledger.

I was learning that although Papa was good at sums, it wasn't his favorite bookkeeping task. Although I knew he checked behind me, he was giving me more and more sums to do in his ledgers.

I didn't mind doing them. Sums, like most things, came easy to me.

Nonetheless, I was still cross with him. Papa had never said anything to me about getting married. A couple of times after men asked him for my hand, he'd asked me if I had any interest in being courted by them.

I never did and he always simply sent the men on their way.

Now he was telling me I needed to get married. Not only that, but he was blaming it on Mama.

Mama was on the other side of the country in Savannah. She didn't know what things were like here. She hadn't even seen me since I'd grown up.

All Papa had to do was to tell her that I didn't need a husband. That I was doing just fine without one.

And now that he'd declared my need for a husband, he'd sent me back to work on the books that he could very well do himself. Away from any man of marriageable age that I might meet.

The stranger who had come in for a glass of water and a room was the first man of marriageable age that I had seen in... well... a long time.

There were men, sure. Most of them were older. Or widowed. There were always eligible carpenters who came in from Denver to work. They work here for the summer, then they'd go back to Denver for the winter.

Or farmers looking for someone to live with them on their farms or their ranches.

I was not that kind of girl. I was a small-town girl. Granted, Whiskey Springs was just a small town, but it wasn't a farm or a ranch where there were no other people around.

Without other people around, I would go stark raving mad. I'd be one of those women being sent back east to the insane asylum.

If Papa ever decided that I needed to spend my days back here trapped in the office, doing bookwork all day long, I didn't know what I would do. He wouldn't do that though. He knew I liked working about among the customers.

I knew the regulars and their families. I asked about them and made them feel at home.

I was an asset. Not someone to lock away in the back office.

But maybe it was a better alternative than getting married.

It wasn't that I was opposed to marriage so much as I was opposed to leaving the saloon.

The saloon was supposed to be mine. I had no brothers. No siblings at all. It had to fall to me. Not now, of course. I didn't wish anything ill on my father.

But in the future. So far into the future I couldn't even see it.

Mama would come back and we would be a happy family again.

She'd been gone so long, I could barely remember the sound of her voice. I only remembered what she looked like because I had a black and white photograph that had been taken of the three of us just before she left.

A photographer had come through town and Papa had insisted that we have our photograph taken. I was beholden to him for that.

Mama would be older now, though. Nine years older, in fact. I couldn't imagine my mother being older.

Maybe I would travel east and visit her. I was old enough now to travel by myself. I didn't need my father's permission.

That's what I would do, I decided, if he persisted with this nonsense about me getting married.

As I finished writing down the last column of sums, it

occurred to me that Papa must have someone in mind for me to marry. This wasn't coming out of the blue.

I set the ink pen aside and looked out the window at the people passing by on the street. Men on horses. Family in wagons.

Father had gone and done what fathers had been doing since the beginning of time. He had gone and found a man for me to marry.

Well. I slammed the ledger closed before the ink even had time to dry. I wouldn't do it.

I wouldn't marry some man just because my father deemed him to be a good match.

Probably some wealthy man. Probably a widower with children. Someone who would "take care of me."

I didn't need to be taken care of. I had the saloon.

I took care of myself.

When my father came to the door, I stood up and put my hands on my hips.

"Who is he?" I asked.

"Who is who?" Papa ask, standing in the door, looking at me with a perplexed expression.

"Who is the man you think I should marry?"

"What makes you think that?" he asked, but I saw the guilt on his face.

"Who?"

"Mr. Pembroke. He owns the General Store."

"I know who he is." And I had been right. Mr. Pembroke was a widower. With children.

"He needs someone to help him out in the store. To do his books for him."

"And he has three children."

"Yes. He does. It's hard for him to keep up with the children and the store."

"So he needs a bookkeeper and a nanny. He can hire someone to do those things."

"Yes." Father nodded slowly. "But a man needs a woman at his side."

"You don't have a woman at your side."

"Bite your tongue, Amanda," Father said in a tone I'd never heard him use with me. "I have your mother."

"She's not here," I said, but I said it cautiously, afraid of my father's anger for the first time in my life.

"I put that man in Room one. See if he needs anything." Without another word, he turned and stalked off.

I waited until I heard him back in the saloon, moving around with the clink of glasses.

"I won't do it," I said, knowing he couldn't hear me. "I won't marry Mr. Pembroke."

I refused to marry a widower with children. Especially a widower who wanted me for being a nanny and taking care of his store.

I had a terrible thought. A thought I wish I hadn't had. But it was there and now I couldn't let go of it.

Father was teaching me how to do the books so I could marry Mr. Pembroke and take care of his ledgers.

"I won't do it," I said, setting my jaw. Papa couldn't make me. If he tried to make me marry Mr. Pembroke, I would get on a stagecoach and travel east to see Mama.

I wiped the ink off my fingers and went out to see what the stranger staying in room one needed.

At least he was a young, handsome man.

If Papa wanted me to marry someone, he could at least look at someone young and handsome.

Chapter Six

SHAWN

I stood in my room and looked around.

The barkeeper was right. It had a good view. Windows to the east and the north. I had a good view of not only downtown, but also the tall, rugged snow-capped mountains.

The sound of hammers seemed to come from every direction, disturbing the otherwise peaceful sounds of the piano music drifting upstairs.

My sister and her husband's cabin was somewhere out there in the middle of nowhere. I'd visit her, of course, one weekend when I was between books, but right now my fingers were itchy with wanting to start the next book.

Although the view was extraordinary, the room was basic. It

had the usual. A bed with clean sheets that smelled like lavender and a clean patchwork quilt that someone had spent hours working on. A wash basin on a table. A lantern. It even had a chair.

Someone had even brought up my trunk. Probably the barkeeper.

But, of course, it did not have a desk.

Rooms never had a desk.

It would give me an excuse to talk to Amanda.

She had vanished after she'd gone to fetch her father to assign me a room.

I pulled out my pocket watch. I had an hour before suppertime. That was an hour I could use to get ahead on some writing.

I sat down on my trunk and used the bed as a desk. Couldn't begin to count the number of times I'd worked like this, especially in the early days before I'd learned to procure a desk for my room.

It had been an older woman in Durango who had hammered that home for me.

"Always ask for a desk. Someone in town will always have some kind of desk you can use. Pay them extra if you have to, but always ask."

So I did. And she was right. Someone always came up with a desk. The funny thing, to me was, they never asked me what I wanted a desk for. I would have asked.

It was one of those peculiar requests that not too many people asked for.

Sitting on my trunk, I pulled out a fresh sheet of paper and setting up my inkwell, I started a new story.

Amanda owned the saloon. She had inherited it from her father and she ran a tight ship.

I stopped and frowned at the words. I was off to a rocky start.

I couldn't stop thinking about Amanda—the real one.

So I went with it.

Amanda had the look of a goddess. Long brunette tresses, red lips that turned a man inside out when she smiled at him.

But it was those eyes. Those mesmerizing green eyes that brought a man to his knees.

There. That was more like it.

I couldn't understand why the first part of a part was always so hard. It seemed to me like now that I had written hundreds of them, it would get easier.

It did not.

The words flowed easily once I got started, but it was the first couple of chapters when I was learning about the characters that took me so long to get wound up.

When I looked up again, someone just outside by window, near the saloon door, was ringing a dinner bell.

I had written five pages of a new novel and it was only Saturday. Maybe I was getting a little faster.

I straightened up the bed turned workstation, capped my inkwell, and washed up to go downstairs for supper.

I'd no more than opened the door when I heard the loud sounds coming from below.

The hammering, I realized had stopped, and the men had come inside for supper.

The girl playing the piano played louder and the louder she played the louder the men talked.

When I got to the bottom of the stairs, I looked around for an empty table. There were none. The men had come in from outside, filling every possible space. Most of them already had plates heaped with food in front of them, served by two women.

The dinner bell, it seemed, had been an afterthought. I would have to remember to come down earlier tomorrow.

I checked the time on my pocket watch. It was ten after six. I would be early tomorrow. I couldn't imagine where they got enough food to feed all these men. Someone had been cooking for hours.

As I stood there, contemplating what I was going to do, Amanda, the real life goddess herself, swept toward me, grabbed my arm.

"Come with me," she said.

Since she apparently wasn't giving me a choice, I let her drag me through the crowded room toward the back of the saloon.

I wasn't going to complain. She could drag me wherever she wanted and I would go happily.

We stepped through a door into what looked like a sitting room with a huge fireplace that opened out into the kitchen.

So this was where all the food prep was done. There was one man, a tall, trim black man doing it all.

"You can sit here," Amanda said, steering me toward a little table for four in between the kitchen and the sitting room.

"Curtis," she said. "Please make sure Mr...?"

"Richard."

"Mr. Richard has plenty to eat."

"Will do, Miss Amanda. Now get out of my kitchen."

Amanda grinned, but she didn't exactly leave the kitchen. Instead she sat down across from me.

"Papa asked me to check in on you," she said, pouring water from a pitcher and sliding it over to me. She seemed to pour the water automatically. Probably did it a hundred times a day and barely even looked at what she was doing.

"Is there anything you need?" she asked.

"Actually, yes. I need a desk."

"A desk? Whatever for?"

There was a first time for everything and this was the first time anyone had asked me why I needed a desk.

"To write on," I said.

"Most people come down during the day and use one of the tables if they need to do any kind of writing."

"I like to write in my room."

She bit her lower lip as she seemed to consider.

"We don't have a desk for guests. My father has a desk in his office, but it's huge and there's no way he would give it up."

"It's okay. I'll look around town tomorrow. Someone always has a desk."

Curtis set a full plate of biscuits and ham and potatoes in front of him.

"Just remember you can use any of the tables. After breakfast, there's hardly ever anyone here."

"I'll keep that in mind. Thank you Amanda."

"Is that all you need Mr. Richard? A desk?"

"I'm a simple man."

"Very well. Enjoy your supper."

As she moved to stand up, I put a hand over hers.

"Stay," I said. "Keep me company."

Out of the corner of my eyes, I saw Curtis watching our interaction as he kneaded biscuit dough.

She sat back down and I released her hand.

"Please accept my apologies," I said. I mostly stayed to myself and seeking out the company of women was not something I did. I didn't want entanglements and having two sisters of my own, I respected women enough to not dally with them.

I figured when the time was right, I'd find a girl I liked and marry her. But I liked my lifestyle and knew that taking a wife would cause innumerable problems.

"No need to apologize," she said.

"I'm accustomed to eating alone. I don't know what came over me."

"I'm sure it's just my charm," she said with a smile that made me glad I was sitting down, otherwise that smile would have taken me to my knees.

"I'm certain that's it," I said. "Please. Call me Shawn."

"Very well, Shawn. You can call me Amanda."

I laughed. "What's your last name Amanda?"

"Amanda Gray."

"Well, Amanda Gray. How long have you lived out here?"

One of the waitresses came into the kitchen, picked up a platter of biscuits and took off with it without so much as a glance in our direction.

"I've lived here my whole life."

"Really? All seventeen years?"

"Nineteen." She straightened in her chair.

"The fresh mountain air," I said. "Must keep you looking young."

"They say I take after my mother."

"Oh?" Where is she?" I glanced over my shoulder, expected to have my ears boxed.

"Savannah."

"Georgia?"

"Yes. She's taking care of her mother."

"I see. So it's just you and your father?" No beau? No husband?

"Just us."

"Miss Amanda?" Another of the waitresses came to the door. "Can you come out for a minute? Answer someone's questions?"

"Of course." She looked back to me. "Will you excuse me?"

"Duty calls."

She looked at me with her head tilted to one side before she stood up and, without another word, followed the young waitress out of the kitchen.

I watched her go, the lovely girl in the lovely emerald green dress, her skirts swaying as she walked.

I reminded myself that I was a nomad. No home. Just roaming from place to place.

I needed to put Miss Amanda Gray out of my mind and focus on the Amanda I had made up for my next story.

That lasted about two seconds.

Chapter Seven

AMANDA

My cheeks felt warm as I went out to see what the problem was in the restaurant.

Whenever my presence was requested, there was sure to be a problem.

Turns out it wasn't so much a problem as it was an annoyance.

"He's been asking for you Miss," Sarah said, nodding in the direction of table with a man and three children.

It was Mr. Pembroke with his family of three. I recognized him immediately. I wasn't sure of Mr. Pembroke's actual age, but I was fairly certain he was at least thirty-five. Balding at the back of his head, he had gray hair wrapped around his head and smoothed down just so. I couldn't remember ever seeing him without a hat and it was hard to keep from looking at his hair. It was wrapped so intricately.

"Sarah said you were looking for me," I said, keeping a smile on my face. "Is there a problem?"

"We just wanted to say hello," Mr. Pembroke said.

"I see. Well. Hello." Always the gracious hostess. "Hello Missy. Ava. And Betsy."

The girls, all under age ten said "Hello" in chorus. It sounded rehearsed. As though Mr. Pembroke had tutored them on what to say.

"Won't you sit for a few minutes?" he asked. "Join us for supper." It didn't sound like a question. It sounded more like a demand.

What was it tonight? Was there a full moon?

"I can't," I said. "working."

"I'm sure your father can spare you for a few minutes. Everything seems to be under control."

Everything appeared under control because I made sure of it. It did not just happen automatically.

"I don't want to intrude. Besides, you don't have a chair."

Without hesitation, Mr. Pembroke pulled his youngest, Betsy, into his lap. Patted the chair where she had been sitting.

"There's a chair now," he said.

"I suppose a minute wouldn't hurt," I said, mostly to myself before I slid into the empty chair.

"You work too hard," he said.

"I don't think that's possible, Sir."

Sitting here, on eye level with him, I actually studied him for the first time, trying not to look at his hair.

He was definitely somewhere in his thirties. Much too old for me.

And there was something about his eyes that put me on edge. When he looked at me, he looked at me from head to toe and back up again. He was, I realized, assessing me just as I was assessing him.

He was a slightly pudgy man. A little big around the middle. The skin above his beard had some pock marks that weren't obvious until we were at eye level. His fingernails needed trimming, too. I felt sorry for the child in his lap.

"Will you eat something?" he asked. "You're skinny as a rail."

"I've already eaten," I lied. I wanted to spend as little time sitting here at his table as possible.

What was Papa thinking? He couldn't just foist me off on some man just because the man needed help. There had to be another reason.

I honestly didn't care to find out.

"Can I get you anything?" I asked, looking for any excuse to be away from here.

"I'd like another biscuit," Missy said, with a lisp between missing teeth.

Bless her heart.

I jumped up from my chair, somehow not toppling it over.

"I'll be right back with that biscuit," I said.

Actually I would send Sarah back with a platter of biscuits that would keep them busy.

I had plenty of other things to do.

As I headed toward the kitchen to find Sarah, I caught sight of Papa watching me with a faint hint of disapproval. I kept walking.

This was worse than I had feared.

What was wrong with Papa? Trying to marry me off to that man who made me recoil?

Ducking into the kitchen, I went straight to Curtis.

"Can I get a plate of biscuits?"

"It'll be ten minutes," Curtis said.

I made a sound and turned around in a circle, one hand pressed against my brow, barely glancing toward Shawn who was watching me.

"Miss Amanda," Curtis said, smoothly. "Sit here. Tell me what's happened."

"It's nothing," I said, but I sat down anyway on a stool at Curtis's worktable. Curtis rarely allowed anyone to sit at his worktable while he cooked.

"Don't look like nothing."

I shook my head. I couldn't tell Curtis about my father trying to marry me off to Mr. Pembroke.

It was too private. Too personal. And so bizarre I couldn't bring myself to voice it.

I lowered my gaze and looked over at Shawn from beneath my lashes.

He'd already finished eating and was sitting back in his chair, watching me.

The difference between Shawn and Mr. Pembroke was alarmingly striking.

If Papa wanted me to marry, it seemed reasonable to think he would encourage me to marry someone like Shawn. Not an old man with long gray hair swirled around his head in a poor attempt to disguise his baldness.

Curtis checked on the biscuits, opening the door of the big iron stove, his hands wrapped in mittens.

"Not yet," he said, moving to his other task of peeling apples for apple pie. Curtis was one of the busiest men I knew.

"I'm still listening," he said. "whenever you're ready to talk."

"I can't," I said, but Curtis made it tempting. It would have been so easy to confide in this older man I'd known since I was a girl. He would have offered me some advice, maybe even a solution.

But I needed to work this out for myself.

First of all, no matter that Papa wanted me to marry Mr. Pembroke, it wasn't going to happen. I couldn't imagine any world in which I could see myself becoming that man's wife.

I'd never defied my father, but he had never asked me to do anything unreasonable. Marrying Mr. Pembroke was unreasonable.

Feeling restless, I got up. Paced to the door leading out to the restaurant.

Mr. Pembroke and his girls were still there.

"Sarah," I said, stopping the waitress as she came through the door. "Would you take a platter of biscuits out to Mr. Pembroke when they're ready?"

"Of course," Sarah said.

"Thank you, Sarah."

I had to get away. I needed to think.

Without even so much as putting on a shawl, I slipped out the back door.

I could go to my cabin, but hiding out there wouldn't solve anything. Besides, I still had things to do.

I had responsibilities.

Pacing along the porch that extended from one end of the building to the other, I rubbed my arms. I didn't leave the porch.

I knew what kind of dangers the night held. Bears. Wolves. To name a couple.

The back door opened and someone stepped outside. I twirled on my heel, my skirts swirling around me, fulling expecting to see my father.

He would scold me for being outside at night alone. That didn't bother me. I knew he was right about that. Papa was right about most things.

That's why I couldn't understand what had come over him.

But it wasn't Papa at the door. It was Shawn.

And Shawn was holding my shawl.

"Thought you might be cold out here," he said as I walked toward him, continuing my pacing route.

"Curtis sent you out here," I said, taking the wool shawl and tossing it over my shoulders.

"Only because I insisted."

"Huh."

"He seemed worried about you."

Shawn fell into step beside me as I continued to pace along from one end of the building and back.

"He shouldn't be."

"So it's normal for you to come outside in the cold night air without your shawl."

I gave him a look and kept walking.

"I take that as a no. You seem agitated."

I stopped and looked at him.

"How can you tell? We only just met."

"I observe people."

"So you watch people and you write a lot."

"What makes you say that I write a lot?"

"You told me," I said. "Besides you have ink on your fingers."

"Seems I'm not the only one who observes people."

"I would think not." I started walking again, only to stop went something moved in the leaves. "I think I'll go back in now."

A twig broke and a snuffling noise came from the darkness.

"Good idea."

Together, we turned and went back inside.

I might be agitated at my father, but that was no excuse to be eaten by a bear.

And Shawn, handsome as he was, didn't look like the kind of man who could kill a bear with his bare hands.

Chapter Eight

SHAWN

I sat in front of the big oversized fireplace in one of two comfortable armchairs.

In between the two chairs was a knitting basket, filled with two balls of blue yarn and one ball of white yarn. Someone was working on something using the blue yarn.

Amanda sat in the other chair.

She was still wrapped in her shawl, even though the flames in the hearth threw off more than enough heat to warm the room and we were sitting right in front of it.

She'd gone from pacing to sitting perfectly still, her brow furrowed.

Something had happened after she had led me back here to the table in the kitchen. It had happened after one of the waitresses had called her out into the restaurant.

Getting her to talk about whatever had happened was proving to be impossible.

"Do you knit?" I asked.

"No." She wrinkled her nose as she glanced over at me. "The yarn belongs to Ophelia."

I hid a smile. Most women enjoyed some kind of needlework. This one seemed to see the question as an insult. My own sisters knew how to embroidery, but they didn't take much time to do it anymore. There were too many other things to do just to survive.

That survival mode had started during the war and it followed them out here to the west. Both of my sisters chose to live out away from town. Sometimes I understood the appeal. The quietness of the night. The bubbling of the stream that they called a river.

Having spent most of my childhood living on the banks of the muddy Mississippi River, it was still hard for me to think a stream I could throw a rock across as a river.

But people out here called the clear water tumbling over the rocks, making them smooth as glass, streams.

I'd gone fly fishing once. For the experience. I preferred to get my fish from a restaurant. Besides, it seemed like my time could be better spent doing other things. Like writing.

"Why do you write so much?" Amanda asked, circling back around to the ink on my fingers. "Do you have family back east?"

"No. Well. Technically yes. But I don't write to them. I have two sisters out here and sometimes I write to them."

"Sometimes."

"I write for a publishing house back east." I didn't go around telling people that I was a writer, but I didn't try to hide it either. People often wondered why I holed up in my room so much. They understood a lot more when they found out I wrote books for a living.

"What do you write?"

"Stories," I said.

She was looking at me with her brow furrowed again, but at least for the moment, she seemed to have forgotten to be agitated.

Leaning over, she dug in the knitting basket and pulled out a thin paperback.

"Like this?" she asked.

I took the novel from her and after studying the cover, fanned through the pages.

"Yes," I said. "Exactly like this."

"Frontier Fantasies by S. Richard," Amanda read, looking over my shoulder. "You wrote that?"

"I must have," I said.

She held out a hand and I gave it back to her.

"You don't know?" she asked.

I shrugged.

Amanda opened the book and started to read.

"Charlie knew he was in trouble when the bottom fell out." She stopped and looked at me. "The bottom of what?"

I laughed. "I remember that book now. It starts off with a rain storm."

"So this is one of yours?" She turned it over. Read the back, then thumbed through the pages much as I had done.

"So it seems. I rarely see the covers or even know what title they give them."

"You don't title your own books?"

"Sure I do. But publishers do what they want to do after they buy it. Sometimes they change the name and then they put a cover on it. Sometimes they even put a different author's name on them."

"That doesn't sound the least bit fair," she said, closing the book and resting it in her lap.

"How many have you written?" she asked.

"I'm not sure."

"Two or three?"

"Hundred."

"You've written a hundred?" she looked at me with disbelief.

"Two or three hundred."

Still holding the book, pressed against her chest now, she sat back and closed her eyes.

"This has been a very strange day," she said.

"What started it?" I asked. "The strangeness?"

"My father."

I felt like we were finally getting somewhere. Maybe she would open up to me now.

"That's a bit vague."

"I can't talk about it."

We sat in silence for a few minutes. The fire crackled in the fireplace. The piano music competed with the voices coming from the saloon/restaurant.

The iron stove door creaked as Curtis opened it to pull out an apple pie, then put in another one.

"How many pies does he make?"

"He makes them as long as people eat them," Amanda said, her eyes still closed.

"Miss Amanda," Sarah, one of the waitresses called from the doorway. "Your father is looking for you."

"Tell him I went home."

"Yes ma'am." Sarah left without batting an eye.

"Can I walk you home?" I asked.

She opened her eyes then and looked at me.

Her green eyes locked onto mine, and I could all but see the thoughts churning wildly in her head.

"Maybe," she said, but made no move to stand up.

"What are you going to do about your father?"

"Unfortunately, he'll find me. I don't have to do anything."

"He knows you didn't go home."

"I don't walk home in the dark alone. It's not safe."

"What will he do?"

"Probably lock me in the dungeon."

My protective instincts kicked in automatically until I realized she was being funny.

"You know," I said. "I'm fairly creative. If you tell me what your problem is, I can help you figure out a way to fix it or at least to get around it."

"There's only one way you can fix my problem," she said.

"What's that? What can I do?"

"You can marry me."

There were some words that universally frightened a man even if the thing itself wasn't frightening.

Amanda had just uttered four of those words.

Chapter Nine

Amanda

Why was it the only men who wanted to get married were the old ogres while the young handsome men looked at marriage as a death sentence?

I had only been jesting, at least for the most part, when I suggested that Shawn marry me.

In truth, I didn't want to marry anyone, but the only way I could think of to truly convince my father to leave me alone about marrying Mr. Pembroke was for me to marry someone else.

Shawn had asked, after all.

Still. I didn't know where the words had come from.

It had to be something about Shawn that had me saying things I normally wouldn't say. Maybe it was the way he looked at me. He seemed... safe.

He was a stranger, but he had a kindness about him that drew me to him.

"Okay," Shawn leaned forward, his hands clasped on his knees.

I understood his ink stained fingers now. If he had written hundreds of books, then the ink would probably never completely fade from his skin.

After I wrote a letter to Mama, it took several days for the ink for wear off my own hands. Papa called me a messy writer. It wasn't my fault that ink got all over my hands when I wrote. I'd had a tutor once who explained that it was because I wrote with my left hand. Personally, I couldn't see why that would matter, but it obviously did.

"Tell me why it is that you find yourself in need of a husband."

I leaned back in my chair, closing my eyes again.

I tried to think of some reason why I shouldn't tell him.

Ultimately, I couldn't come up with a reason.

As he said, he might could help me. And, truly, it was a little too late now. I had already told him what I needed. It seemed only fair that I tell him why as well. An explanation seemed like the proper thing to offer.

Opening my eyes, I looked into his blue eyes. Blue like a clear summer sky.

"Papa has decided that I need to marry."

"So it isn't you who has decided you need a husband."

"Goodness no. I don't want to marry anyone."

"Generally, when a father wants his daughter to marry, he often has a reason. Does your father have someone picked out for you to marry or is it just a general sentiment?"

"He has someone picked out." I looked away, into the fire.

Trying not to visibly recoil at the memory of Mr. Pembroke's hair wrapped around his balding head and his dirty fingernails that needed to be trimmed.

"Is he... someone you would like to marry?"

I looked at Shawn askance. "If he was someone I would like marry, I would hardly have a problem, would I?"

"You make a good point," Shawn said, rubbing his chin. "Did this come up suddenly?"

"Today." I wrinkled my nose. "I never paid the man in question much attention. He was recently widowed, so why would I? But tonight... He wanted me to sit with him." I shuddered. I couldn't help it.

Shawn hid a smile behind his hand.

"It's not funny," I said, but I suppose it sort of could be funny if it were anyone other than me.

"It's quite serious, actually," Shawn said. "But you amuse me. So don't take my amusement the wrong way."

"Are you married?" I asked, suddenly curious about this man.

"Me? No. I move around too much."

"You don't have a home?"

"No. I guess I don't. I guess I always considered my sister's home to be mine."

"But you don't actually live there?"

"I visit."

"A man without a home would not make a good husband."

Shawn laughed.

"It's funny you would say that when only minutes ago, you proposed to me."

"I did not propose to you," I said, keeping my shocked voice low.

"Right," Shawn said. "You just said you needed a husband and I should marry you. Or something to that effect."

"I don't need a husband," I said, feeling weary. "My father thinks I do."

"Miss Amanda," Curtis called from his stove behind us. "The pie is ready to serve."

"Please excuse me," I said. "I need to help the waitresses serve apple pie."

"By all means." He stood up as I did.

"Would you like some pie?" I asked.

"Only if you will have some with me."

"Alright," I said. How could I refuse a gentleman's gentle request for sharing a slice of pie?

"Just watch out for *him*."

I looked at Shawn a moment, then I realized he was talking about Mr. Pembroke.

"Don't worry. I'll keep my distance."

Chapter Ten

SHAWN

With pie being served, things got busy in the saloon again.

Curtis's pie, it seemed, was in great demand.

I didn't see how one man could peel and slice enough apples to make pie for the two dozen or so customers who eagerly waited.

I watched Amanda take charge of the two waitresses. Making sure they got everyone served. Amanda, however, didn't just supervise, she also served some slices of pie to customers herself.

It was all quite efficient.

While I sat in my chair in front of the fireplace, an older woman, probably mid-thirties, wearing a plain white dress, came and sat down in the chair Amanda had left vacant.

"Hello," she said as she picked up a skein of blue yarn from the basket between the two chairs and began knitting.

"Hello. You must be Ophelia."

"Yes," she said with a smile. "I am. How did you know?"

"Amanda told me the yarn belonged to Ophelia."

"You have a good head on your shoulders," she said. "A good memory."

"Thank you."

I settled back and watched the flames flickering as it devoured the logs in the oversized fireplace.

"You seem like a good man," Ophelia said, nearly startling me, we had been sitting quietly for so long.

"I like to think so. I come from a good family."

"I can tell. So does Amanda."

"Yes ma'am."

Her fingers still methodically moving the knitting needles, she looked at me with watery greenish blue eyes that almost seemed transparent.

"She's not one to be dallied with." She looked deep into my eyes as though she was trying to see my intentions or perhaps even to see into my soul.

"I'm not one to dally with women."

"Good," she said, turning her attention back to her knitting.

Relieved that her attention was no longer focused on me, I glanced over my shoulder, hoping Amanda would be back soon.

"You should marry her," Ophelia said.

"Excuse me?"

"She's a good girl. Smart. Well-bred. She'll make the right man a good wife."

"I can see that she would." I took a deep breath. "But I'm not searching for a wife."

"Shawn," she said. "Sometimes a wife finds you."

Finding her words disturbing, I looked back into the flames.

"I have our pie," Amanda said, coming toward me. I stood up to take the two plates from her.

"Thank you," she said, moving toward her seat.

"You can take my seat," I said, turning.

"What?" She sat down in her chair—the same chair Ophelia had been sitting in only a moment earlier—and held out a hand for her plate.

I handed her one of the two pie plates and slowly sat back down in my chair.

"Nothing," I said.

The blue yarn was back in the basket, just as it had been before Ophelia had sat down.

"Are you okay?"

I nodded and tasted the pie with fresh apples and flaky crust.

"Curtis makes a good pie," I said, still feeling a bit off-balance. "Does Curtis make pies every day?"

"Only on Saturdays and any day he deems a special occasion."

"I see."

It wasn't just what Ophelia had told me. That I should marry Amanda and that "sometimes a wife finds you." But it was that she had simply vanished so quickly. She must have dropped her knitting needles and whatever it was she was knitting back into the basket. Just looking at it, I couldn't even tell that it had been disturbed.

Perhaps I needed to get some sleep. I'd had a long day. A long couple of days, actually, traveling.

I just needed a good night's sleep.

As I sat there, eating my pie in silence, I realized that Ophelia had known my name.

Chapter Eleven

Amanda

Shawn ate his pie in silence. I wondered if he was one of those moody men who could go from friendly to distant with no apparent reason.

I hoped not, but I couldn't see any reason why he would suddenly be so quiet.

I didn't normally eat pie, so it was a treat for me and I was determined to enjoy it.

Not only did I not normally eat pie, I also didn't normally take time away from helping out in the saloon.

Tonight, however, I had my reasons for staying in the back. First of all, my father was tending the bar and, feeling cross with him, I was avoiding him.

Second, Mr. Pembroke was out there with his three daughters, expecting me to return to his table to join them. I was avoiding him, too, and for good reason.

In fact, I might never go back into the General Store again, seeing as how he owned it.

I still couldn't fathom what my father was thinking in suggesting that I marry that man.

I wasn't supposed to get married. I was supposed to inherit the saloon. To own the saloon and run it.

That, the way I saw it, was my destiny.

Mr. Pembroke might live here in town, but he was no different from any other man in that he would take me away from the saloon.

My father had gone daft.

And now Shawn thought the same thing about me.

He'd probably had time to think about our conversation and was ready to be away from me. I didn't blame him. He thought I had proposed marriage to him.

I'd been around men enough to know that men didn't consider marriage until they were ready. But from what I had observed in my work at the saloon, once a man decided to take a wife, he didn't hesitate to do so. He'd set his sights on a woman and they would marry in no time.

On the other hand, a man who was not ready to get married would avoid it all costs. I even knew of one man who had left town to avoid marriage.

Penelope Smith had set her sights on the man—his name was Henry Drake. After about a week, Henry had packed up his things and left town. No one had heard from him again.

Penelope was a spinster now at the age of twenty-one.

I did not want to be like Penelope.

I would be horrified if my comments to Shawn sent him away. He not only seemed like a good man, I found him interesting. I'd like to know more about his writing.

"I want to apologize for our earlier conversation," I said.

Shawn looked at me now, for the first time since I had gotten back to my chair.

"Why would you apologize?"

"I don't want you to think you have to leave town because of me."

Shawn set his empty plate on the floor next to his chair.

"I don't understand."

"I'm not setting my cap for you or anything. I am simply trying to avoid Mr. Pembroke."

"You have every right to avoid Mr. Pembroke," Shawn said, obviously confused.

"You just seem quiet and well. I wanted to apologize."

"I was just trying to make sense of something."

"Oh. Good."

He reached down and lightly touched the blue wool.

"What is it you were trying to make sense of?"

"Ophelia," he said. "She seemed..." He stopped himself, then seemed to go in a different direction. "She knew my name, even though I can't possible figure out how."

"Ophelia knows everyone," Amanda said. "She was here?"

"She was sitting right there in your chair. Knitting. Then she just sort of vanished."

Amanda nodded slowly. "She talked to you then?"

"Yes. She was quite pleasant, but opinionated."

"Don't worry about her. She's harmless."

"She was knitting," Shawn said again, looking down at the wool in the basket.

"She's making a scarf, I think. For her husband."

"I see."

"He was a soldier in the Northern army."

"The war?"

"Yes."

"The war was over years ago," he said, with obvious puzzlement.

"I don't think that matters to her."

"You said he was a soldier."

"He never came home. His was killed at the battle of Antietam."

"And yet she's still making a scarf for him."

"When she got the letter, it broke her heart."

"She did seem rather sad."

"Shawn," Amanda said, shifting in her chair to face me. "Ophelia is a ghost."

Chapter Twelve

SHAWN

I'd been a young boy when the war broke out. I'd seen a lot of things in those ten or so years.

On the day my oldest sister, Ember, had gotten married, her new husband had been called to fight in the war. He had never come home.

Ember had traveled west to live in a cabin that her husband had built for her. Coming west alone had taken a huge leap of faith on her part.

After the war, her husband had returned.

That had been nothing short of a miracle.

After the war, my other sister and I had traveled west on our own. Our parents were supposed to join us later, but they had yet to do so.

She was married also. So both my older sisters were married.

Left to my own devices, I had taken to traveling and writing.

And although I had seen a lot of things, I had never, to my knowledge at least, seen a ghost, much less had a conversation with one.

It was most disconcerting.

"How do you know?" I asked. "Have you seen her? Have you talked to her?"

"No." Amanda looked away toward the flames in the hearth.

"Then how do you know she's a ghost?" I reserved the right to remain optimistic that Amanda was mistaken.

"Everyone knows," she said. "But only a few people have seen her." She lowered her voice. "I think Curtis has seen her."

Curtis was a black man. It didn't surprise me that if there was a ghost, he had seen her. Growing up in Mississippi, I was well familiar with the black culture and their familiarity with voodoo and other supernatural phenomenon. It had never frightened me. It was just the way it was.

In fact, if Curtis had seen Ophelia, I was even more inclined to believe that I had seen her as well. I was more inclined to think that Ophelia really was a ghost.

"What happened to her?" I asked. The Ophelia that I had met was not that old. Not nearly old enough to have died of old age. Probably my mother's age now, even though it was odd to think of my parents aging, even though I hadn't seen them in neigh onto ten years.

"They say she died of a broken heart," Amanda said.

"Is that what you think?" I asked. "Do you think it's possible to die of a broken heart?"

"I think so," Amanda said, thoughtfully, looking at me. "Do you?"

"I think it's possible," I said. "But the women in my family are strong. I don't think it would happen to just anyone."

I thought about my sister Ember who had come west alone after believing her husband was killed in the war. I thought about my other sister, Olivia, who had traveled west with me. Olivia'd had horrific nightmares that had only resolved after her now husband and I had defeated a man who had been after him for something that had happened in the war.

The four years of war may have only been a short time in the great scheme of things, but it had left an indelible scar on the country that I feared would never heal.

Brother against brother. Neighbors killing neighbors merely because they wore the wrong color. The war wasn't something that was likely to soon be forgotten, if ever.

Too many good men had died. And that was just on the battle-field. No one would ever know how many people had died on the home front from starvation and disease and deserters from both sides.

But even with the horrors of the war, I believed that people could love so deeply that their hearts could be broken.

"I think if I had to marry Mr. Pembroke, I would die of a broken heart," she said.

"I think if you married Mr. Pembroke, I would die of a broken heart."

Chapter Thirteen

Amanda

A fight broke out in the saloon. Not unusual for a Saturday night. The men had tomorrow off and so they had no reason not to let off some steam.

Letting off some steam, however, often, like tonight, led to fighting.

The men usually fought over one of two things. Cards or women.

Needless to say, there weren't enough women for the men brought in from Denver during the summer months to do construction. Some of them brought wives or other relatives, but for the most part there was a dearth of women as compared to the men of Whiskey Springs.

I was sometimes surprised that things stayed as peaceful as they did.

I was looking at Shawn, absorbing his words about dying of a broken heart if I married Mr. Pembroke when the outburst started.

I stood up automatically, even though I knew my father would handle the situation. He always did.

Shawn stood up, too, and moved to stand in front of me, surreptitiously blocking my path to the main part of the saloon.

Even though I knew there was nothing I could do when a fight broke out among the men, I felt compelled to investigate.

When a gunshot rang out, I froze.

I'd worked in the saloon alongside my father for a long time and never once had I encountered a gunfight.

Gunfights were something that happened in the dime novels that Shawn wrote. They weren't something that happened in real life to real people in thriving little western towns.

Most people out here were helpful and kind and overall just good people.

But that had most definitely been a gunshot.

"Stay here," Shawn said, turning and heading toward the saloon.

I followed, of course, stopping at the door to take in what was going on. The first thing I noticed was that the piano was quiet. Mandy, currently on piano shift, had ducked beneath the piano.

Most of the men had moved out of the way, standing along the walls and some even ducked behind the bar.

Two men stood face to face and one of them held a pistol.

But they weren't looking at each other.

They were looking toward the bar.

Time seemed to be frozen in that moment. The seconds stretching into minutes until time had no boundaries.

Then everything was moving again.

The sheriff grabbed the gun from the man holding it and led him outside.

A couple of men rushed toward the bar.

I looked for my father, but didn't see him.

Maybe he had stepped outside for a few minutes. That would explain why the altercation had gone as far as it had.

It was only after time had started to flow again that I realized someone behind the bar was injured.

I moved forward without thinking, somehow instinctively knowing that someone had been shot.

Just as instinctively I knew that the person who had been shot was my father.

Maybe I didn't know it as much as I dreaded it.

Someone said my name.

"He's been shot."

"Someone get Doc."

"Where's Amanda?"

Then I was rushing behind the bar, seconds later, kneeling next to my father.

"Papa!" It didn't take much of a quick search for me to find the blood on his shirt.

"He's been shot." I echoed the words I'd heard someone else say. "Papa."

He was unconscious. With panic ripping me apart, I discovered that the blood was coming from his shoulder.

With fear rushing through me, I grabbed hold of a thread of relief that the bullet hadn't hit his heart or his stomach.

Someone handed me a cloth and I pressed it against the wound to stop the bleeding.

"Doc is on his way," someone said.

I was vaguely aware that Shawn was there with me, kneeling on the floor next to my father.

"Let me," he said, ripping Papa's shirt away from the wound and using his own strength to stop the bleeding. "He's going to be okay."

I heard the words. I don't know that I believed them. I was afraid to believe them. I was afraid not to believe them. But I held onto them.

After what seemed like forever and yet was probably no time at all, Doc was there, shooing us all away.

"Get him to my office," Doc said. "I've got to get the bullet out."

Standing back, watching in horror as three men picked up my father and hauled him out of the front door of the saloon.

My father was not a small man. He was tall and he was muscular, but they carried him with ease. That frightened me as much as anything. It seemed as though his blood was seeping out, making him lighter.

I followed them outside into the night air.

When the coolness of the night breeze hit my skin, I realized that my eyes were moist and damp with tears.

Looking over my shoulder, I realized that Shawn had not come outside with me. I'd wanted him to. Expected it even. But I didn't have time to worry about him right now.

We reached Doc Alexander's office and then I was standing in the waiting room staring at a closed door. The men dropped Papa off and came back out, leaving Papa alone with Doc and his wife who worked as his assistant.

I was aware of all this happening somewhere in the back of my mind, but the only thing I could focus on, really, was my father. He was behind the closed door with Doc and there was nothing I could do to help him right now.

Pacing, I waited. My hands trembled and my knees were weak, but I kept pacing. I couldn't sit down. I couldn't be still.

Mrs. Alexander came out and stood in front of me. She wore an apron over her pretty blue dress. The apron had blood smeared on it. My father's blood.

"He's going to be okay," she said. "The bullet made a clean wound. Doc is stitching him up now."

"Is he awake?" I couldn't stop looking at the splatters of blood on her apron.

"He was, but Doc gave him something for the pain. So no. Not now."

"Can I see him?"

"In a few minutes."

"How did this happen?" I asked, mostly to myself.

"The sheriff said it was an accident."

When had she spoken to the sheriff?

Time wasn't fitting together in a normal fashion for me right now.

"You should go home," she said. "Get some sleep."

"No," I said. "I have to see him."

"That's what I thought you'd say. Come with me."

My father was lying there on the bed. They had cleaned up the blood, bandaged him up, and covered him with a clean blanket.

Sitting down in the chair next to the bed, I took his hand and just held it while he slept.

I was vaguely aware of Mrs. Alexander and Doc moving around the room, taking care of things. Cleaning up. Checking on Papa.

But I focused only on my father. Willing him to wake up. Willing him to be okay.

Chapter Fourteen

SHAWN

I shut the saloon down at Midnight.

It wasn't without protests, but everyone complied when I announced that I needed to close up.

Even though I knew I could have closed up the bar right after Mr. Gray was carried out and the shooter was taken out of the saloon by the sheriff, but the men needed to have a drink. To process what had happened.

No one questioned me when I stepped behind the bar and began pouring drinks and collecting payment for them.

There was too much confusion for one and second, people were willing to follow a man who presented as being in charge. I'd learned that a long time ago.

When Mr. Gray and his daughter were suddenly no longer

available to run things, someone had to step up. I figured I was as qualified as anyone to step up and handle the business part of the saloon.

Maybe it was presumptuous, but I liked Amanda and I couldn't bear the thought of people taking advantage of the situation. Not that they would take advantage intentionally.

But men would be men.

Since the saloon was also a hotel, one that I was staying in, I couldn't just lock the front doors.

I found a key to a cabinet and locked up the liquor, putting the money I had collected in the cabinet with it.

I slid the key in my pocket and went outside. This was one of those times when sleep had to be forfeited.

It didn't take me long to find Doc's office. It was the only building with a faint light glowing through one of the windows. It was most likely also Doc's home.

What Mrs. Alexander referred to as the hospital room was on the first floor. I wondered when she slept. Perhaps she was like me, foregoing sleep when necessary.

Then I heard an infant's cry and understood part of the reason why she was awake. It was not just for her patient. It was also for her baby.

I found Amanda, sitting in a chair next to where her father lay sleeping in a bed, holding his hand. She was bent over, her head resting on the bed, using her arm as a pillow, and she was asleep. Mr. Gray appeared to be sleeping peacefully.

The small room was filled mostly by the one-person bed— little more than a cot really. A wash basin stood next to the bed and there was a shelf with clean linens and a tray of medical devices on it. I recognized scalpels, scissors, and a bone saw. That was the thing about being a writer. I knew a little bit about a whole lot of things, but was an expert in nothing except maybe putting together a good story.

A window was cracked an inch or so, letting in the night sounds. Crickets chirping and a wolf howling somewhere across the valley. Beneath it all was the gentle roar of the rushing little river.

Ever so quietly, I pulled a wooden chair from a corner of the room and sat down next to Amanda.

I gently swept a lock of hair off her cheek. Even in sleep, her brow was furrowed with worry.

I longed to touch her smooth skin, but had to settle for gazing upon her full red bow-shaped lips and long dark eyelashes that smudged the area beneath her eyes.

I didn't want to wake her. While her father healed, she slept. It was how they both would get through this unnecessary tragedy.

I don't know how long I sat there with nothing but the soft glow of a candle breaking the darkness.

Chapter Fifteen

AMANDA

The next morning, responsibility beckoned me back to the saloon.

I'd sat with Papa most of the night and I stayed with him as long as I could. I stayed with him until he opened his eyes and asked me what I was doing there.

"You should be at the saloon," he said. "Who's watching after it?"

I didn't bother to tell him that only yesterday, he had tried to marry me off so I could watch after the General Store. Who would watch the saloon then?

But he looked too fragile lying there and even though there was no version of my world where I would marry Mr. Pembroke, my anger at my father had dissipated.

I walked across the street in the brisk morning air. The scent of burning firewood mixed with the strong scent of new growth from the spruce trees. I could smell a rain shower coming, too, making the spruce scent even stronger.

The streets were deserted, but the dueling hammers blended with the steady clang of the blacksmith's iron tools.

I walked past the stables I hadn't even noticed last night in the frenzy of following my father to Doc Alexander's office.

Half a dozen horses stood grazing in a corral behind the simple one-story barn with large double doors that stood open to let in fresh air. A young boy carried a saddle almost bigger than he was. I missed a step, almost stopping, wondering how that had happened when his father came out into the corral behind him.

"I can do it," I heard the little boy say. His name was John and his father's name was Martin.

"I know you can, Son," Martin said. "but let me help you lift it up onto this horse."

I kept walking, the normalcy of everything catching me off-guard. In my world, my father lay fighting for his life, everything was turned upside down. But out here the rest of the world carried on as though nothing had changed.

Out here this was just another day. A normal day.

Reaching the saloon, I opened the two wooden doors, securing them back on either side of the traditional swinging doors.

Stepping inside the saloon, for the second time in less than a handful of minutes, I missed a step.

I had expected the saloon to be deserted and quiet. Only now I realized that someone was at the piano playing the uplifting music that lured people inside. The music had been so normal I hadn't even noticed it until now.

We never locked the doors because the saloon was also a hotel, but there was no one to run the bar itself.

Curtis was good in the kitchen, one of the best cooks, but he didn't know alcohol and he didn't know how to count money.

I smelled biscuits and bacon and three tables were filled with customers having breakfast.

Then I saw someone behind the bar.

I stopped right there among the tables. My heart pounding too fast, causing me to feel a little bit dizzy.

Then the man turned around and my heart flipped the rest of the way over.

I reached out and put a hand on the back of an empty chair at the nearest table to steady myself.

Shawn stood behind the bar, wearing a white apron, looking all the world like he belonged there. A visceral reaction. That's what I was experiencing. I had to be careful. Shawn working in the saloon was an anomaly. Not something I could allow myself to think of as normal.

"Shawn," I said, with a quick glance around.

One of the waitresses, Shelley came out the kitchen, carrying a tray piled high with food.

"Miss Amanda," she said with surprise to see me. "How is your father?"

"Resting," I said. "Healing."

"We were all so worried," she said. "I prayed for him last night."

"Thank you, Shelley," I said, forcing a half smile.

As Shelley continued on her way to deliver the tray of food, I continued on my way toward the long mahogany bar.

"Hey," Shawn said, coming around and taking me by an elbow and leading me toward the nearest empty table. "Sit down." He pulled out a chair with his other hand and I dropped into it.

"I'll be right back," he said. He went to the kitchen door, said something to Curtis, and came back, sitting down in the chair next to me.

"You must be exhausted," he said.

"I am. What are you doing here?" I asked.

Curtis came around the corner, carrying a tray balanced on one arm and a pitcher of orange juice in his other hand.

He set everything down on the table. Two glasses. Two plates heaped high with food.

"You need to eat, too, Mr. Shawn," Curtis said as he poured orange juice into the glasses. "You both had a long night."

I looked curiously at Shawn, trying to figure out why Shawn had a long night.

"Much appreciated," Shawn said.

After Curtis left, I picked up my glass of juice and quenched a thirst I didn't know I had.

"What did he mean by that?" I asked.

"I don't know," Shawn said. "I guess he knows everyone was worried."

"Oh." I stared at the plate of food in front of me, replaying last night in my head.

"I'll eat if you will," he said, pulling me out of my memories.

"Okay." I shook myself. I didn't have the luxury of wallowing in unpleasant memories. I had responsibilities.

We ate in silence for a few minutes. I was most definitely hungrier than I had thought.

"Why are you here?" I asked again, realizing he hadn't answered me earlier.

"Just looking after things," he said. "Curtis has the kitchen covered, but someone needed to be behind the bar.

"You didn't have to do that. I expected the bar to be closed. Papa has someone who helps out, but he wasn't scheduled."

"I know," he said, finishing up his meal. "But I've got this. If you want to go home. Get some sleep, you can rest knowing the saloon is in capable hands."

"How do you know how to run a saloon?" I asked.

"Sometimes a writer has to work for his lodging."

"How is it you've written so many books and you still have to do other work?"

"It's been awhile," he said. "but things were lean when I first started out."

"I'd rather be here," I said. "helping out."

"You're asleep on your feet, Amanda," he said. "Please. Let me walk you home. Get some rest before you're in Doc Alexander's other bed."

He was right, of course. I'd slept some last night, but not nearly enough and not nearly comfortably enough, sleeping sitting in a chair bent over with my head on the bed.

I had the momentary sense that Shawn had been there with me, but I shook it off. If he'd been there, I would have remembered it.

Chapter Sixteen

Shawn

It was easy to slip into old habits.

In fact, it was only Monday, so I slid into the old habit like sliding into a well-worn pair of boots that fit my feet perfectly.

I sat behind the bar, helping people when they needed it, getting them drinks, asking Curtis to bring them food. When there was no one who needed anything, I wrote. I had a stack of paper, my inkwell, and a pen set up at the end of the bar. Not a bad work area.

No one seemed to notice or care that my fingers were stained with ink.

Amanda came into the saloon in mid-afternoon when I was right in the middle of a gunfight scene. I set my paper aside, knowing I could easily pick it back up.

"Hey," I said. "How's your father?"

"He's much better. Ready to get out of the bed which Doc says is a good sign. Thanks for sending over the tray of food."

"I figured you would be hungry and he needed to eat."

"He did eat. I'm feeling much better about his recovery."

"Good to know." I went back to wiping down the bar and straightening bottles of whiskey. They said that was how Whiskey Springs got its name. The saloon never ran out of whiskey.

Amanda went around and started wiping down glasses.

"I'm going to have to start paying you," she said.

"I don't want you to pay me. I'm just helping out."

"You can stay for free then."

"If you insist," I said. "But I had something else in mind."

"What's that?" she said absently, opening the cabinet where I was stashing the money in a box. "I need to work on the books."

"A picnic. Let me take you on a picnic."

She straightened and turned to look at me.

"I'm sorry. What?"

"It's a sad state of affairs when a young lady works so much she doesn't even think about going on a picnic."

"You want to take me on a picnic? Why?"

Here I was giving her a hard time about never going on a picnic when I was basically in the same state. The last time I'd been on a picnic, it had been with my sister Olivia and her husband.

That, actually, was the day I decided to start traveling. I didn't like being their third wheel.

So here we were. Two peas in a pod.

I didn't court anyone because I traveled around too much. She wasn't courted by anyone because she worked too much.

"What are you smiling about?" she asked.

"Just thinking. I should have asked you if you had a beau first."

"I don't have a beau," she said. "Unless you count Mr. Pembroke."

"We were having such a good conversation," I said.

She laughed, then bit her lip.

She was a pretty girl, but when she laughed, her whole face came alive with a beauty like none I had ever seen.

"Okay," she said. "I won't count him."

"Thank God," I said. "I thought for a minute I was going to have to challenge the man. And truth be known, it would not go well for him."

"Are you secretly a famous gunfighter?" she asked.

"Yes. Actually. My real name is Buck Montana and the very sight of me strikes fear in the heart of men everywhere."

She smiled.

"Can I get a whiskey?" A burly man asked, sliding onto a bar stool.

"Of course," I said, taking a glass and filling it with whiskey before sliding it over to him.

"You do a good job of keeping your true identity a secret," Amanda whispered as she walked behind me.

I laughed.

"What's going on out there?" I asked the burly man sitting in front of me. The hammering had all but stopped.

"A rain storm," he said. "You're about to get busy."

I looked out the front window. I hadn't even noticed the dark clouds that had moved in, bringing wind and rain wasn't far behind. As I watched, lightening flashed and thunder quickly followed.

Such was the way of the real world.

As much as I was enjoying spending time talking with Amanda about nothing in particular, she and I were about to get slammed with a whole bunch of carpenters getting an unexpected day off.

Chapter Seventeen

AMANDA

While Shawn tended the bar, I ducked into my father's office to do some bookkeeping.

A thunder storm crashed all around us, keeping the saloon filled with men who would otherwise be outside building. I could barely even hear Bailey on the piano, there were so many men talking all at once. So instead of dueling hammers, the air was filled with conversation and rain pounding against the glass at the windows.

It was a little strange being in my father's office without permission. It was his private space. Always had been.

Any time I'd been here I had been here at his specific request, whether to add columns of numbers or look at whatever else he wanted to show me.

Lately though, he'd shown me enough about how he kept records that I knew what to do.

I sat at his big oversized wooden desk, working by the light of a lantern.

I enjoyed the distraction, the satisfaction even, of working with numbers and having the columns balance out. I enjoyed it enough that it distracted me, at least for a while, from worrying about my father.

It did not, however, keep me from thinking about Shawn.

Just knowing he was out in the saloon, behind the bar, was comforting.

He wanted to take me on a picnic. I couldn't help but wonder where that came from. It seemed out of the blue. Maybe he was trying to cheer me up by getting me out in the fresh air, away from work, away from everything that came with worrying about my father.

Even if we didn't go on a picnic, just thinking about it was distraction enough in and of itself.

I'd been working on the books close to three hours when I realized I needed to look back at a purchase Papa had made last winter, but it wasn't in the ledger I was working on.

I went to the shelf where he kept his books and quickly found what I was looking for. Fortunately, Papa was quite organized.

I found what I was looking for, but something didn't add up.

Taking the ledger with me, I went back to the big oversized desk and sat down. I was still trying to sort it out when Shelley came to the door.

"Miss Amanda," she said. "It's getting awfully busy. Do you mind helping us out for a little while? No rush."

"Of course I don't mind," I said." I need a break from all this anyway."

I shoved the ledgers aside and stood up, straightening my skirts. I considered dashing home to brush my hair, but I reminded myself that I was going out to work in the saloon. Not to impress Shawn.

Still. I straightened my hair before stepping out of the office.

My gaze went straight to Shawn and he chose that moment to look up, his own gaze landing right on mine.

It nearly took my breath away.

Feeling a little weak in the knees, I fisted my hands in my skirts and walked straight into the kitchen.

"There you are," Curtis said. "Just in time."

"You always say that," I said, picking up the tray he had ready to be served.

"And it's always true. You have good timing."

I rolled my eyes and carried the tray out into the chaos. What was it about rainy weather that made people want to get out of their houses?

Chapter Eighteen

SHAWN

The rain settled in for the night. I wondered if it was possible that the storm got lodged between the tall mountain peaks surrounding the little town and just sat over us, unable to move.

It didn't work that way, but it certainly seemed like it did. I liked the idea so much I started thinking about just how I could use it one of my books.

First I had to finish up the gunfight I was writing. Maybe I'd use the storm in next week's book. That was the great thing about writing a new book each week. I seemed to have a never ending supply of ideas and the books gave me a place to put them. It baffled people and was something I certainly couldn't explain. I didn't even try anymore. I mostly just shrugged and told them it was a hazard of the trade.

That usually confused people enough that they stopped asking questions I couldn't answer.

The saloon was busy, mostly with the carpenters who got an unexpected day off. Toward suppertime, however, families started to wander in, shaking out their wet cloaks and hanging them by the door. Some even used umbrellas. The wall was lined with half a dozen of them, water pooling on the floor. My theory was that people, no matter how much they complained about bad weather, liked to get out in it. They would stay inside for days, but when a thunder storm settled in, they had to get out.

I didn't mind the rain. I actually found it to be soothing.

With the rain and the steady work at the bar, writing during the lulls, it was a pleasant way to spend an afternoon. Amanda was the only thing missing.

She spent the afternoon in her father's office working on his accounts. Even though I knew she was back there, I missed her and looked toward the office a few times more than I probably should have.

When things got busy at suppertime, Shelley, one of the waitresses asked Amanda to come out and help her.

I caught a glimpse of her as she walked past toward the kitchen.

Seeing her walk past was like catching a glimpse of a ray of sunshine breaking through the clouds.

Something had come over me when I was talking to Amanda earlier today. Going on a picnic was not something I had ever asked a girl to do.

Maybe it was the clean mountain air that had me thinking

about walking outside, sitting on a blanket beside the river, and just watching the clouds roll by.

"I haven't seen you around here before," a young lad around twenty-years-old said as I slid his drink across the bar to him.

"No sir," I said.

"My name's Nickolas."

"Pleasure to meet you Nickolas," I said. "My name is Shawn."

I smiled as Amanda picked up a couple of drinks I had waiting for her to deliver to tables.

"Be careful with that one," the young man said.

It took me a moment to realize he was talking about Amanda.

"What do you mean?" I wasn't one to listen to gossip, but his words startled me.

"She's a nice girl, but don't try to get too close."

I didn't respond to that. I wasn't even sure I wanted this man's opinion on Amanda. I had already formed mine anyway.

I refilled whiskeys for two other men sitting at the bar, glad for the excuse to distance myself.

The man's glass was soon empty, however, and I was obligated to head back in his direction.

"Didn't mean to offend you," Nickolas said. "It's not Amanda that's the trouble. It's her father. She's had at half a dozen marriage proposals and her father turns them all down. Acts like she's some kind of princess or something. Too good for any of us local men."

"Good to know," I said, at a loss for anything else to say.

If nothing else, talking with Nickolas was a reminder of one reason I liked cities and only stayed in small towns for short periods of time. In small towns everyone tried to get into everyone else's business. It was okay if a man was passing through, but a man who decided to settle somewhere became the object of gossip.

If Nickolas had been one of those men proposing to Amanda, I could see why Mr. Gray had refused to give his blessing.

Besides, I knew for a fact that Nickolas had wrong information.

Mr. Gray had in fact accepted a proposal of marriage from Mr. Pembroke, a man Amanda most certainly did not want to marry.

Something wasn't adding up. Not that it was my business, but it was a puzzle begging to be solved.

Chapter Nineteen

AMANDA

When Shawn announced that the bar was closing at Midnight, I didn't argue.

The rain was still falling, but the men needed to get some sleep. Tomorrow the rain would surely be out of here and they would need to get back to their hammering and sawing.

When I'd seen Nickolas sitting at the bar, I had steered clear of him. He was one of those men I hardly even knew who had asked to marry me. Nickolas hadn't asked me. He had gone straight to my father.

I found that rather odd.

It would have been a lot more efficient if he had asked me if I was at all interested before he went to the trouble to ask my father.

Papa had asked me what I thought and I had told him.

I had told Papa I didn't want to get married. I wanted to run the saloon.

How many times had I told Papa that?

And yet now he wanted me to marry Mr. Pembroke.

Maybe now that he had been shot, he understood how crazy an idea that was. Or he might be even more convinced that a bar is a dangerous place, especially for a woman.

Whichever it was, he would have to get past it.

It was still pouring down rain after everyone was out of the now quiet saloon.

No one was around except for Curtis who was already peeling some potatoes to cook for breakfast. Curtis was always at work.

I stood at the big window at the front of the saloon and looked outside, watching the rain fall.

"I'm not looking forward to getting out in this," I said, going back behind the bar.

"Then don't," Shawn said as he locked the cabinet where he was keeping the money.

"Unfortunately, all the rooms are booked, so I don't have anywhere to sleep."

"Take my room," Shawn said.

"I can't do that. Where would you sleep?"

He looked around a minute, seeming to consider.

"The floor," he said.

"I can't ask you to sleep on the floor."

"You didn't ask. I volunteered."

I shook my head. "Thanks, but that wouldn't be right."

Right on cue, a rumble of thunder shook the entire building.

"I can't let you go out in this. Your father didn't ask me to look out for you, but I think he would have if he'd gotten the chance."

"You feel responsible for me?" I asked.

"I guess I do."

I wasn't sure what I thought about that. I had mixed feelings.

Nonetheless, I knew he was right. It wasn't safe going out in this weather. Getting struck by lightning was right up there with being eaten by bears or wolves.

"Okay," I said. "You win. But not on the floor."

"What do you suggest then?"

We'd finished our work and stood behind the bar looking at each other.

"I don't know, but there has to be a solution."

"Agreed."

"Come on. I'll walk you up to my room."

Once again, I found his easy charm hard, no, impossible to resist.

After locking up Papa's study, I walked upstairs with Shawn. He carried a lantern to light our way.

We stepped into his room and the door closed behind us.

I looked over at Shawn, my eyes wide.

None of the doors in the room closed automatically. I knew. I'd been in all of them. When I was younger, I had helped clean the rooms in between guests.

Shawn hadn't closed the door. He was standing next to me and he looked just as surprised as I did.

He didn't hesitate to step over and put his hand on the doorknob.

I watched him turn the knob and he even shoved against the door, but it didn't open.

"It won't open," he said, giving me a baffled look.

"Let me try," I said, stepping forward.

The door didn't open for me either.

"How did it lock from the outside?" I wondered. "The lock is here on the inside."

"Maybe it's jammed," Shawn said, setting down the lantern and trying again.

"The weather," I said, but it was more of a question.

"Maybe. A prank?"

"Who would do that? And why? We didn't pass anyone in the hallway."

"Good point." He ran a hand through his hair and scratched his head. "Beats me."

The wind howled, shaking the windows on one side. With this being a corner room, there were windows on two sides of the room.

Shawn went to one window, then the other, checking to make sure they were closed. He put his hands behind the back of his head and looked at me with a shrug.

"It has to be the storm," he said.

"It has to be," I said, but I wasn't convinced. "What are we supposed to do?"

"I guess we'll sleep here."

She glanced at the little bed and shot me a look.

"I'll sleep in the floor," he said, going to the bureau and pulling out an extra blanket and a pillow.

He made a pallet for himself on the floor not far from the door.

Then he looked at me with obvious satisfaction.

"See?" he said. "Simple solution."

I rubbed my eyes. I was really tired.

This was so improper on so many different levels. And yet there was nothing I could do about it.

With a sigh of resignation, I dropped onto the side of the bed.

There was no way I was going to get any sleep tonight. Not with Shawn here in the same room.

But since I was stuck here, not just from the rain, but also from the locked door that shouldn't be locked, it would be a good place to spend the night. Maybe I could at least get a bit of rest.

By morning, we would find a way to get out of this locked room, surely, and I could go home. Get a few hours of sleep.

It was a good plan, I decided, all things considered.

Seemingly satisfied with the situation, Shawn sat on his pallet and pulled off his boots.

I looked away, feeling the heat rising in my cheeks.

Sitting here on Shawn's bed, even with him on a blanket on the floor, seemed entirely too intimate and highly inappropriate.

"Do you mind if I turn out the light?" he asked.

"Please do," I said. At least with the light out, we wouldn't be able to see each other.

He turned the knob on the lantern, putting us in total darkness.

I sat there a moment, then put my feet on the bed and lay my head on the pillow.

I would just rest for a bit.

And while I was resting, I used the time to go through all the possibilities of why the door would be locked from the outside and just how we might get it open.

Chapter Twenty

SHAWN

The wind howled outside and rain splashed against the windows. Being on the corner, there was plenty of glass for the wind and rain to slam against.

Without the light from the lantern, we were in total darkness, even though the curtains were open. Clouds blocked any moonlight that normally would have come through the windows.

After a few minutes, I heard the rustle of Amanda's skirts as she put her feet up on the bed and stretched out.

I'd taken the liberty of taking off my boots before I even thought about it making Amanda uncomfortable. Her cheeks flushed, she looked away.

Putting out the light seemed like a good solution.

Stretching out myself, I put my hands behind my head and tried to sort out how we got in this situation.

I'd insisted that she stay in my room instead of going out in the storm. There was no sense at all in going outside in this weather. Not when there was a perfectly good room right here where she could sleep.

I accepted the possibility that she might not actually get any sleep. At least maybe she could rest and I could rest easy knowing she was safe and dry. It was probably selfish of me to think that way. The more I thought about it, the more I decided it was selfish.

But it was the best I could do.

We were somehow locked in this room together. We would simply have to make the most of it.

The thought crossed my mind that Ophelia might have had something to do with it, but I promptly dismissed that idea.

A few minutes later, I heard Amanda's breathing relax as she fell asleep. She had the softest, sweetest snore I'd ever heard. I couldn't even really call it a snore. It was more like a steady yawning sound.

At any rate, whatever I might call it, it made me smile.

I would have bet money that she wouldn't have been able to sleep with me in the room. But she did.

Either she was completely exhausted or she trusted me enough to fall asleep. Maybe a little bit of both.

I wanted her to trust me.

Ophelia's words came back to me. *You should marry her.*

Had Ophelia done this? Had Ophelia locked us in this room together somehow?

The next time I saw Ophelia, I would have to have words with her about doing something like this.

I would have been okay sleeping on the floor on the *outside* of the room in the hallway just as easily as I was sleeping in a locked room.

Surely the door would open in the morning. If not, we could beat on it until someone came and opened it.

Not that I minded being locked in a room with Amanda.

Even though I would have bet money that she would be the one who couldn't sleep, it might just be that I was the one who would have trouble falling asleep with her in the room.

Ironic, wasn't it that I would be the one to lie here on the floor unable to sleep?

Amanda was making me think about upending my life.

I let myself imagine for a moment what it might be like to give up my wandering ways and settle down here in Whiskey Springs.

Amanda and I could get a little cabin down by the river. We could still work in the saloon if she wanted to, but we didn't have to.

I had enough money stacked up from my writing that even if I never picked up another pen, we could have anything we wanted and live anyway we wanted to.

I couldn't do that though. Writing was in my blood. It wasn't something I could just stop doing. Besides, I couldn't risk the money running out. We would need plenty of money to send our children to college back east. To get them the best education possible.

My active fantasy mind had taken hold of the idea and I could clearly see our lives together down to the details. We'd have a two-story house with a tall grandfather clock in the foyer, just like we'd had back home.

But I was getting ahead of myself. I would need to channel this fantasy into my next book.

In my next novel, I'd write about a man who married the girl of his dreams. Of course, things wouldn't be easy for them. There would have to be a villain. Someone from his past, or even better from her past.

As I played out plot possibilities in my head as I often did to help myself fall asleep, I remembered what Nickolas had told me.

Amanda's father wasn't about to let her marry anyone, at least not anyone other than Mr. Pembroke, whatever his reasoning.

My fantasy broken, I sighed and let my thoughts drift aimlessly as I listened to the rain splashing against the windows and Amanda's steady breathing.

I needed to keep my mind focused on what I needed to do. I needed to write my books.

Working in the saloon was temporary and wasn't a real job.

Somehow my brain was getting confused.

Chapter Twenty-One

AMANDA

I woke to the sound of birds chirping their morning song.

It was odd, though, because I couldn't hear the rushing river in the background.

Instead, I heard the sounds of a buggy.

I decided I must be still dreaming. In my room, down the path from the saloon, there were no buggies.

Our cabin had no actual road to it. Just a footpath.

Since my father owned the saloon, he didn't need to keep horses and certainly not a buggy at our house.

We didn't even own a horse or a buggy. There was no need. Not when we could walk anyplace we wanted to go.

I lay very still and let myself fall back asleep.

I don't know how long I drifted back into a light sleep, but when I opened my eyes, sunlight was streaming across my face.

The birds were still singing, but I still couldn't hear the roar of the river.

Then once again, I heard the sound of a buggy rolling past. Maybe a wagon.

Slowly opening my eyes, I tried to figure out where I was.

I was not in my bedroom.

I was in one of the rooms on the second floor of the saloon.

It all came back to me in a rush.

I was still sleeping my dress and my shoes, even though I had not planned on falling asleep.

How was it possible I had fallen asleep with Shawn in the room?

Not hearing a sound from him, I sat up and looked across the room.

He was not there. The blanket and pillow were gone as well.

I had not imagined it.

If he wasn't here, had the door unjammed, then?

Putting my feet on the floor, I dashed over to the door and turned the knob. It opened up just like it was supposed to.

I stood there in the open door way and took a deep breath.

Whatever had caused the door to jam last night had resolved itself.

There was no clock in the room, something I resolved to remedy—each room should have a clock—but I had the distinct feeling that I had slept later than usual.

With nothing else to do, I left the room and headed downstairs. I would need to walk to my cabin to change clothes and ready myself for the day.

Someone was at the piano. It was Mandy. I recognized her way of playing. She wasn't our best pianist, but she was reliable and made up for her lack of skill with enthusiasm.

Carefully making my way downstairs, I planned on slipping out the back door. With no mirror, I could only imagine that I must look a sight.

Rumbled clothing and disheveled hair, no doubt.

I would slip out and no one would be the wiser.

If anyone questioned why I was here, I would simply explain that the storm had been too bad for me to go home. It was, after all, the truth.

Perhaps I wouldn't tell anyone that I'd been locked in a room and certainly I wouldn't tell anyone that I'd been locked in a room with Shawn.

My reputation would be destroyed.

Curtis, at work as usual, had his back to me as I slipped past him.

According to the clock on the mantle, it was nearly ten o'clock. I couldn't remember the last time I'd slept until ten o'clock. Sleeping in was a luxury I didn't normally have.

Almost to the door, I grabbed one last quick glance over my shoulder and ran headlong into someone.

Gasping, I would have fallen backwards, except for the strong arms that steadied me.

Blinking and looking up, I saw that Shawn was the one I had run right into.

Shawn. The very person I was trying to avoid, truth be known.

"Good morning," he said.

"Good morning," I said, pulling myself together and lifting my chin.

"Did you sleep well?" he asked.

"It seems I slept too well," I said. "I never sleep in this late."

"I didn't want to wake you," he said, keeping his voice down discreetly, lest we be overheard.

"I'm not sure if I should thank you or not."

"I would probably thank me. You seemed exhausted."

Someone moved around behind us.

"Come," he said. "Let's sit out here on the back porch."

I followed him outside and we sat on a wooden bench.

I swept my skirts aside to make sure he had plenty of room to sit.

Squirrels skittered in the maples trees at the edge of the building, sending little pieces of debris falling to the ground.

"How did you get out of the room?" I asked, now that we were out of earshot of others who might inadvertently overhear us.

"The door just opened. Whatever jammed it, just let it go."

"No idea what it was?" I asked.

He shook his head in a way that told me that even if he did have an idea what jammed he door, he wasn't going to tell me.

"Well. Today is a beautiful day."

The sky was blue with a few wispy clouds. The only evidence of last night's storm was a scattering of limbs on the ground.

Papa was usually the one who would clean up the mess. He took pride in the ownership of the saloon.

"I need to check on Papa," I said, appalled at myself for not doing that right away.

"He's fine. I went by Doc's this morning. In fact, he'll be coming home today or tomorrow."

"Oh. That's very good news." I had to figure out how I was going to watch after Papa in the cabin and watch after the saloon at the same time.

"I hope you don't mind. I took the liberty of hiring a nurse to care for him."

"You hired someone?"

"Yes. Is that okay?"

"Of course," I said. "That was very thoughtful."

I needed to get back to the ledgers to make sure we had the money to pay for a nurse to take care of Papa. And besides that, I had to pay Shawn for taking care of the saloon.

"I can see the worry written all over your face," he said.

"I was wondering how I was going to watch after him and the saloon at the same time. But I need to check Papa's ledgers." Something hadn't been adding up the last time I had worked on them.

"Don't worry about paying the nurse," Shawn said. "I took care of it."

"Shawn. You can't do that. I'm supposed to be paying you."

He brushed a strand of hair off my cheek and shook his head.

"A man doesn't get the chance to help a damsel in distress very often. Please don't take that away from me."

He was smiling at me, looking so very charming, that I found I didn't know how to resist him. What's more, I didn't want to.

I'd let it go, for now at least. Maybe I'd ask Papa what to do about it. Or maybe not. Maybe this was one of those things I had to figure out for myself.

Chapter Twenty-Two

SHAWN

I worked behind the bar for the rest of the afternoon. It was such a pretty day, there were only a couple of customers coming through. I mostly had the saloon to myself.

It was such a pretty day, if I hadn't been so used to spending my time indoors writing, I would have hated it. But I was accustomed to spending my days inside. It's what I did.

I wiped my hands, transferring most of the ink from my fingers to the towel.

I was making progress with my story. I had, inadvertently perhaps, written Amanda into the story as the cowboy's love interest.

That was only natural. I had a feeling I would be using some version or another of her in a lot of stories to come.

I had her—the fictional Amanda—on a carriage, going to visit her cousin in a nearby town when she was set upon by bandits.

Fortunately, my hero had followed her and was close by to save the day.

It was a simple story, really, but it was one of those stories that readers liked. I knew this because it was the kind of story I'd liked as a boy. Plain and simple. Damsel in distress. Saved from bandits by the hero.

The real Amanda, not the one I'd made up in my head, wasn't quite so quick to accept being rescued by me. She was a modern woman whose father owned the saloon. He didn't just work at the saloon, he owned it. That meant that Amanda would be reluctant to ever leave here.

People talked and I listened. It was hands down the best way to learn things.

I soaked up information like a sponge, then it somehow found its way through my fingers, onto the page, usually in an entirely different format. I was the only one who had some idea how it worked.

But when it came right down it, even I had to admit that I didn't know how it happened. All I knew was that when I sat down with a stack of paper and a pen, words appeared on the page.

It was a kind of magic.

Amanda had walked down to Doc's office to get her father ready to be brought home and Curtis was the only other person in the saloon. He was in the back peeling potatoes for tonight's supper. I sat in front, at my stool behind the bar, frantically writing down my thoughts as fast as I could. The bar had turned out to be a pretty good desk and I had managed to go right back into the mode of writing with distractions all around me.

A movement off to my left caught my attention and I turned to see someone standing behind the bar.

My first thought was that Amanda had returned.

But instead, I saw, with quite a start, that it was Ophelia.

She stood there, humming to herself, wiping whiskey glasses with a white cloth.

I stood there, watching her. She was wearing a long blue dress, very demure. Her brunette hair was pulled up and back, falling loosely from the top of her head in soft ringlets.

She acted as though she had every right to be here. As though she actually worked here.

As though she was here alone.

I had a few things to say to her, but in the moment, I found myself unprepared.

My head was still deep in my story and I hadn't thought about Ophelia since Amanda and I been locked in my room.

"It's a slow afternoon," she said, not even looking up.

"Yes," I said. "It's a beautiful day outside."

She went back to humming to herself, not responding to my comment.

It occurred to me that it was quite possible that she didn't even know I was here.

She appeared to be in her own little world.

"Johnathan should be coming home any day now."

"Johnathan?"

"Johnathan is fighting for the North. He's fighting to keep the Union together."

I didn't know if I should answer her or not.

She sat one glass down and picked up another. Began to meticulously wipe it until it shone, all the while humming to herself.

"What about you?" she asked, still not looking up, keeping her eyes on the glass.

"Me?"

"Do you fight for the north or the south?"

"I'm a southerner ma'am," I said. As much as I wanted to play along with her in this conversation, I was a southerner through and through.

Even when I was a youngster, too young to join the army, I wore my little butternut gray uniform and dreamed of the day when I would be old enough to fight for my homeland.

Whether fortunately or unfortunately, the war had ended before that had happened.

"Well," she said. "It's a good thing you're here then. You wouldn't want to meet my Johnathan on the battlefield."

"No ma'am. I would not."

She turned then and looked right at me.

I recognized the nearly translucent watery greenish blue of her eyes. I had to fight the urge to back away from her intense gaze that seemed to see right through me.

I couldn't, in fact, discern if she was looking at me or through me.

Since it was impossible for me to tell, I sat very still and waited to see what she would say next.

She looked so very real, if Amanda hadn't told me that Ophelia was a ghost, I never would have thought it.

I would have just thought she was a very sad looking woman. A little strange perhaps, but strange didn't bother me.

In my travels, I'd learned that everyone was different and people weren't really so much strange as they were different.

I was glad for it, actually. I soaked in everything I could about people so that I could create interesting characters to put in interesting situations.

Ophelia was standing still now, the glass still in her hand, but she was merely holding it.

"You look a lot like my Jonathan," she said.

"No ma'am," I said quickly. "My name is Shawn."

"Oh, I know that," she said, turning her penetrating gaze away from me and back onto the task of shining the glasses, one by one.

She hummed a few more strains and I wondered what I was supposed to do.

I couldn't just leave her here.

"Jonathan promised me he would be home soon," she said.

"I'm sure he'll be home as quickly as he can," I said.

"He's not coming home," she said. "I know that now."

"How do you know that?" I asked.

"I'm wise now," she said. "Wise beyond my years." She laughed a little, without humor.

"I'm certain you are ma'am."I immediately regretted the comment.

She turned and looked at me again with those eyes that saw right through me.

"You're a good man," she said. "You have to stay strong."

"Why do I need to stay strong?"

"When things happen, you need to be strong."

"What things?"

Instead of answering, she turned and looked toward the door.

"What things do I need to be strong about, Ophelia?"

The front doors opened and a couple of men wearing boots and cowboy hats stepped inside. They were laughing and talking.

Feeling an unexpected need to protect her, I stepped toward her.

"Maybe—"

Whatever I was going to say was lost to me.

Ophelia was gone. Vanished. The white cloth she had been using to shine the glasses with lay there in a crumpled heap.

I picked it up and it was warm in my hands. Warmer than it should have been under normal circumstances.

But these were not normal circumstances.

"Can we get a whiskey?" one of the two men asked as they slid onto two barstools.

They didn't look like carpenters or trappers or even farmers or ranchers.

"Of course," I said, setting two glasses on the bar and opening a bottle of whiskey. "What brings you to town?"

"Just looking for a little bit of fun," the other guy—the younger one— said.

Trouble, I decided right there as I poured whiskey into their glasses. They were here for trouble.

Whiskey Springs, it seems, was not the sleepy little town it wanted to be.

Already, the saloon owner had been shot and now these two men showed up looking for trouble.

I could spot it a mile away.

A hazard of the trade.

That's what I would tell anyone who asked me how I knew.

Chapter Twenty-Three

AMANDA

I spent the afternoon of the beautiful day after the storm cooped up in my father's study, my head bent over his ledgers.

With soft piano music drifting from the otherwise quiet saloon, I added numbers and added some more. I added columns of numbers until they all started to swim together in my head.

Finally, I found what I had been looking for.

There it was in the previous ledger I had taken from Papa's shelf. A sum of unaccounted for money. Four figures.

The only notation next to the influx of money was "H.P."

Harold Pembroke.

I didn't understand it. I didn't want it to be true.

It was just my imagination running wild. Papa wouldn't take money from Harold Pembroke. Not without some good reason.

Maybe he had sold a horse. "Horse... Peddling."

Except that Papa had never owned a horse, at least not to my knowledge.

Brushing the end of the ink quill absently against my chin, I tried to figure out what this transaction meant.

There was no logical explanation.

With a sudden terrible thought landing in my head like a rock in the pit of my stomach, I pushed up from the desk and went over to the shelves where he kept his ledgers.

Pulling the next one from the shelf, I began the painstaking process of looking at each transaction. I looked for four figures, but also for large three figures. Even more importantly, I looked for "H.P."

I found another entry exactly three months before the first one I had found. Same amount.

Four figures.

I marked the page with a folded piece of plain paper and kept looking. Column by column.

I needed to find out what my father had done.

As I searched the ledgers, I tried to remember the last time my father had told me that the saloon would be mine when he was gone.

I couldn't remember the last time.

Looking up, I checked the clock on Papa's wall. I had time to go home, where Papa was now, before I was needed out in the saloon, and ask him.

But... somehow confronting him didn't feel right.

It seemed like one of those things that he should tell me about on his own accord.

Maybe that. Or maybe I just didn't want to hear the answer.

"Hi," Shawn said.

I looked up, startled, to see him standing in the doorway, leaning against the door jamb.

"Hi," I said, marking my place and closing the ledger.

"Are you okay?" he asked.

"I think so," I said, notwithstanding the queasiness in my stomach. Actually he looked a little shaken himself. "Are you?"

"Not really."

"Why not? What's happened?"

He sat down in one of the two oversized chairs across from Papa's desk. At first he didn't say anything. He just looked straight ahead.

"I saw Ophelia again," he said finally.

"Just now? Where?" I looked toward the door, halfway expecting to see her there, having followed Shawn.

"Behind the bar. She was wiping glasses with a cloth."

"Like... working?"

"Yes. It was so very odd. I think she knows she's a ghost."

Sitting back, I gave this some thought.

"Why wouldn't she know?"

"I don't know. The first time we talked, she didn't seem to know. But just now she did. I can't explain it."

"I'm really glad I've never seen her," I said with a little shiver.

"She's not that old. Pretty. But her eyes are so sad."

"A ghost with sad eyes," I said. "You can write about that in one of your books."

"Yes." Shawn smiled a little. "I suppose I can."

Our eyes met across the desk, tripping my heart rate into a dangerous rate.

"Do you want to take a walk?" he asked. "Before it gets dark?"

I did. I wanted to very much. But...

"Who's watching the bar?"

"Curtis."

"Curtis? He doesn't know what to do. He's not trained."

"I trained him." Shawn looked rather pleased with himself.

"You did not."

"I did."

"But Shawn," I said, lowering my voice. "Curtis can't count money."

"He can now. I taught him."

Well. If anyone could teach anyone anything, it would be Shawn.

"Okay," I said. "A walk sounds nice. I was just thinking I need to check on my father." Or something of that nature. Close enough.

Shawn stood up and held out a hand. "Shall we?"

I smiled and put my hand in his.

It felt so very right to have my fingers linked with his.

When it came to Shawn, I was very much in over my head. All I could do was follow my instincts.

When it came right down to it, it didn't occur to me to do anything else.

Chapter Twenty-Four

SHAWN

It was a beautiful evening for a walk.

Last night's rain had left everything clean and fresh smelling. Mostly the spruce trees. Nothing was more refreshing than spruce trees after a rain.

The setting sun splashed a rainbow of colors across the sky.

I wondered if Amanda could paint. Walking along beside her, her hand in mine, I wondered about a hundred things about her.

I would learn them in due time. There was so much to learn and I wanted to know everything about her.

It was important to take my time, to get to know her slowly. All in due time.

We walked beneath a grove of maple trees with new growth sprouting out on the branches.

As we neared the creek, known around here as Whiskey Springs River, its rushing waters became louder.

The path down to Amanda's house was a pleasant walk through the forest.

Two chipmunks dashed across path, then shot like bullets up one of the white barked aspen trees.

I could get used to living here. It was a lot like where my sister Olivia lived, but it might be a bit prettier here. I was reserving judgment on that.

Whiskey Springs was surrounded on all sides by tall, sky scraping rugged mountain peaks. Their ruggedness was offset by caps of soft white snow.

"What are you thinking about?" she asked.

"Nothing much," I said. "Just noticing how pretty it is out here."

"Papa says it's one of the prettiest places in the country. I've never been anywhere else, except Denver a couple of times, so I couldn't say."

I nearly missed a step. It hadn't occurred to me that Amanda had never been anywhere else. She'd been to Denver, so that was something. But there were so many beautiful places. It was hard to imagine that she had never been anywhere but here.

"It is one of the prettiest places I've seen," I said.

"You've traveled a lot." she said. "You must have seen a lot of different places."

I nodded. "I have seen a lot of different places from here to Wyoming and back. I want to see Montana, but I haven't made it yet."

"How long do you think you'll stay here?" she asked. "Before you move to the next place?"

"I honestly don't know," I said. "I usually stay at least a week in any one place. It works well for my schedule. Then I go to the next place. Or not. It just depends. During the winter, I usually stay put for the season."

"I see."

We were nearing her house. She and her father lived in a two-story log cabin that hardly looked like a log cabin with its wide front porch with two wooden rocking chairs sitting side by side.

It looked settled. Like it had been there for a long time.

"Is that the nurse's horse?" Amanda asked.

"I don't think so. The nurse would walk."

Besides the big dapple gray had a man's saddle on it.

"I wonder who's here," she said.

As we neared the cabin, I could feel the tension running through her.

"It's probably just someone coming by to check on your father," I said, wanting to alleviate some of that tension.

"Probably," she said, but the tension remained.

She hurried her pace, going up the four front porch steps to the door. She didn't hesitate. Just threw open the door.

"Should I wait?"

But she was already inside, dashing across the foyer, bringing me with her.

She stopped at the entrance to the parlor where her father sat on the sofa, his face pinched, his shoulder bandaged.

But it wasn't her father that was the problem.

Mr. Pembroke stood at the fireplace mantle, a glass in his hand, looking all the world like he owned the place.

"Papa?" Amanda said, looking to her father for answers.

"Come in," Mr. Gray said. "Join us. Take a seat."

Amanda hesitated.

"I can just—" Go ahead. Be anywhere but here.

But Amanda just held my hand all that much tighter.

I could only imagine how this must look.

The man her father wanted her to marry stood right in front of us and she was holding my hand.

I had to remind myself that this wasn't one of my novels where everything was melodramatic.

In my books, I would soon be facing Mr. Pembroke in a misty meadow at daybreak. Our backs to each other as we paced apart, only to turn and fire upon each other. One of us dying there on the grass of the meadow.

That might be a made-up outcome of this situation, but according to the way my stomach felt right now, it might as well be real.

I was all about melodrama in my book, but in real life, there were certain things I preferred to avoid.

"What's going on?" Amanda asked. "Why is he here?"

"Amanda," Mr. Gray said. "Please sit down. It's time I explained everything to you."

She sat down on the edge of the sofa with obvious reluctance. I sat next to her with equal reluctance and managed to pull my hand from hers with what I hoped was a great deal of discreetness.

It wasn't that I was afraid of either one of the men in the

room. It was that in my real life, it was my preference to avoid drama.

"Who is he?" Mr. Pembroke asked, looking pointedly at Shawn.

"This is Shawn. He's been watching after the saloon while Papa has been recovering."

Mr. Pembroke grunted.

"He's been a great deal of help to us," Papa said.

Mr. Pembroke looked away, obviously dismissing me as not important enough to concern himself with either way.

I was here now. And if Amanda needed me to be here, that was good enough reason for me to stay.

Ophelia's words came back to me, unbidden. *When things happen, you need to be strong.*

Chapter Twenty-Five

AMANDA

The grandfather clock in the foyer steadily ticked away the minutes as I sat next to Shawn, waiting for my father or even Mr. Pembroke to tell me what the meaning of this was.

Papa took a cigar from a box on the table next to his chair and took his time lighting it. I was probably—hopefully—the only one who noticed his hands shaking.

I would not have been so concerned if it hadn't been for the notations in the ledgers indicating a steady influx of money every three months. Notations with nothing more than the initials "H.P."

Something was not right.

If the initials referred to Harold Pembroke, something was most definitely worse than not right. Something was very wrong.

"I have something I need to tell you," Papa said after taking a steadying drag from his cigar.

"Is this about the money?" I asked. Despite my earlier decision to not confront my father on the ledger entries, the situation had changed.

I had very little patience left for any matter involving Harold Pembroke. Having the man standing in my house, acting every bit like he owned the place was the last straw.

"Yes," Father said. "I should have told you a long time ago."

I looked over at Mr. Pembroke. At the thin gray hair swirled around his head to hide the baldness beneath it. It was all I could do to suppress a shudder.

"What have you done, Papa?"

Papa winced as he straightened. I felt bad for him, but I was also angry with him. Angry and wary.

"You wouldn't have any way of knowing this," he said, "but the saloon business isn't what it used to be."

"What do you mean? We're always busy."

"We have a lot of expenses," Papa said.

Mr. Pembroke went over to the sideboard and poured himself another glass of whiskey.

I had to bite my lip to point out the expense of him drinking Papa's whiskey.

Instead, I crossed my arms and raised an eyebrow at my father, ignoring Mr. Pembroke's bad manners.

Father seemed to back up and start over.

"You know I miss your mother," he said.

"We both do."

"I've come to the conclusion that she isn't coming back."

"Why?" I asked, fighting the panic that rose in my throat.

"The situation," Papa said, with a wave of his hand. "At any rate, I've decided to join her."

"You're going east?"

"We're going east," Papa said.

East. Hadn't I just been contemplating going east to be with Mama?

I had been contemplating doing just that, but now listening to Papa, I suddenly most certainly did not want to go east.

I was shaking my head.

"No. Papa. We can't leave here. The saloon."

"That's the thing I've needed to tell you," he said. "I've been selling the saloon to Harold."

"You've... Been..." I look from my father to Mr. Pembroke and back again. "Papa you can't do that. It's our saloon. It's going to be mine someday."

Papa touched his bandaged shoulder with his other hand and confirmed exactly what I'd feared he would be thinking.

"The saloon is not a safe place. I was just standing there. Minding my own business and was shot. I can only imagine the dangers you, as a woman, would face as the owner of the saloon."

"It could have been anyone," I said. "Anyone could have been shot."

"Exactly my point," Papa said.

He and I were using the same occurrence to make different points.

I risked a glance at Shawn. His expression was impassive as he watched the exchange between me and my father. He no doubt saw himself as having no place in this conversation.

"Then why on earth did you want me to marry the man?" I asked, not caring that Mr. Pembroke was standing right there.

"Forgive me Amanda," Papa said. "It was a compromise. It was a way for you to have it both ways. If you were married to Mr. Pembroke, the saloon would still be yours in a round about way."

"Wasn't my idea," Mr. Pembroke said. "And I'm still not convinced." He glanced over at Shawn.

"So you sold him the saloon. And instead of telling me, you decided to marry me off to the man."

The emotion rose in my throat to the point where I could barely speak.

I needed to get away. I needed to get away from my father. I couldn't look at him right now. And I certainly couldn't look at Harold Pembroke.

Without a word of explanation, I got up and dashed out the back door.

It was dusk now. Not a safe time to be outside alone, but I didn't care.

I gathered up my skirts and started to run. I didn't know where I was running. I was just running. I just needed to get away.

I stopped when I reached the river's edge and dropped to my knees.

The hot tears that spilled over my cheeks weren't a surprise.

I needed to talk to my mother, but she was in Georgia. I couldn't talk to her. I could write her a letter, but it could be weeks or even months before she got it.

Besides, that wasn't the same thing as talking to her face-to-face.

Hearing something come up behind me, I merely ignored it.

I didn't care if it was a bear or a wildcat. Right now it didn't matter to me.

I felt like I'd already been attacked by my own father.

Maybe being attacked by a bear would have been less painful.

"Amanda."

It wasn't a bear, though, or a wildcat. It was Shawn.

I wiped at the tears on my cheeks. Even with everything as it was, I didn't want him to see me like that.

He came and knelt next to me.

"What can I do?" he asked.

"Help me understand why my own father turned against me."

Chapter Twenty-Six

SHAWN

"I can't speak for your father," I said, kneeling on the ground next to Amanda. My knees were already soaked from the damp ground.

Rushing water tumbled over boulders in the river in front of us. When the wind turned just so, a light mist touched our skin.

"I know," she said, so softly I could barely hear her over the roaring water.

"But my gut tells me he was trying to protect you."

"By making me marry Mr. Pembroke." She stared at her clasped hands in front of her. I got the impression that she was holding onto her composure the same way she was squeezing her hands together. With all her might.

"Now that I don't understand." Why would a man marry his daughter off to a man like Harold Pembroke? Not only was he far too old for her, he was revulsive to my eye, not just physically either, and I considered myself to be a fairly good judge of character.

"At least it isn't just me," she said.

"No, Amanda. It's not just you."

She turned and looked at me. Her big green eyes and dark lashes were moist from crying.

My heart melted.

Every protective instinct I had coalesced right there onto Amanda.

Her lips parted and my gaze dipped down to her bow shaped lips. I wanted to kiss her now. I could kiss her now.

But she lowered her gaze.

"What do you want me to do?" I asked.

"I don't know."

Water from the river misted over us but the warmth of the sun dried it almost immediately.

"How long has it been since you saw your mother?" I asked.

"I don't know. She left when I was twelve. Seven years ago I guess."

"That's a really long time. You've grown up since you saw her."

"I miss her."

"It was the same for my family. I was really young when they sent me west with my sister."

"Why?" she asked, looking up and searching my eyes. "Why would they do that?"

"The war had just ended. Things were bad. They sent me west

with my sister Olivia. We were supposed to go to live with our other sister Ember."

"I take it you didn't make it to Ember."

"Not exactly. My sister, Olivia, got married instead."

"So both of your sisters are married? But you aren't."

"Not yet," I said. "I haven't felt the inclination."

Not until now.

The inclination struck me all of a sudden. It was so swift and so sudden that I was thankful I was not standing up.

"I don't think I ever want to get married," Amanda said.

And that inclination deflated just as quickly as it had hit me.

"You can go with your father to Savannah to be with your mother."

She stared out toward the rushing water.

"I could. I thought I wanted to. But now I don't want to go."

"You want to stay here."

"I did," she said. "But now I don't think I can even do that if I wanted to."

"Because your father is selling the saloon."

"It looks like, for all intents and purposes, he already has. I don't know how much money Papa has taken from him already, but whatever it is, there's no way I can pay it back."

She couldn't pay the money back... but I could.

I had never aspired to own a saloon. I'd worked in some, sure, before I became a prolific writer, but owning one sounded like a whole lot more than I wanted to take on.

It was an option, though. One that I would keep to myself for the time being.

"I don't know what to do," Amanda said. "I thought I would

stay here and run the saloon. But now... that isn't an option. I don't want to go east. I don't think so anyway."

I took her hands and waited until she looked up, meeting my gaze.

"You don't have to do make a decision right now. Right now you don't have to do anything."

Nodding, she took a deep breath.

I, on the other hand, had a lot of things to think about.

Chapter Twenty-Seven

AMANDA

By the time Shawn and I walked back to my cabin, it was getting dark.

It was the time of day when both the sun and the moon were visible at the same time.

"It's like another world, isn't it?" I asked after Shawn pointed out both the sun and the moon to me. "A made up place."

"It is. But it's real." He squeezed my hand. "Just like this moment."

All sorts of emotions ran through me. Emotions I didn't feel like I could deal with right now, so I changed the subject.

"What's it like making up stories?"

"It's the best job in the world."

"But it's more than just a job, isn't it?"

"It's who I am. I made up stories even when I was a teenager. I thought everyone did."

"That's kinda funny."

"Yeah. That's what my sister Olivia thinks."

"I take it she didn't make up stories."

"No. Just me."

"I don't have any brothers or sisters," I said. "I missed out on a lot, didn't I?"

"Sometimes," Shawn said, shoving a low hanging branch aside as we walked past, sending the fresh scent of spruce needles through the air. "Actually yes. I can't imagine growing up without my sisters."

"You miss them."

"Of course I do, but I wouldn't tell them that."

"You would, too," I said.

"I have a lot to teach you about having siblings. I'm more than happy to share mine with you."

I nearly missed a step. He said the words so easily.

Did he offer to share his sisters with all the girls he met on his travels?

It didn't seem like the kind of thing that would be appropriate to ask. Asking would sound flirtatious. Flirtatious was something I had never been.

Anytime a boy showed any interest in me, Papa would send me to the kitchen.

Curtis said Papa was just trying to protect me.

"We're here," Shawn said as we reached the front porch. "Looks like Harold Pembroke left."

"Thank goodness. I'm going to run upstairs. Change dresses and come right back down."

"Take your time."

"What are you going to do while I'm changing?"

"I might just check on your father."

"Good idea," I said, though the thought of what Papa and Shawn might say to each other made me a little bit nervous.

It was quite likely that Papa would blame Shawn for me not wanting to marry Mr. Pembroke. He should know better than that. I couldn't even imagine what he must have been thinking when he'd decided it was a good idea for me to marry that man. A man—an old man—with three daughters and a general store to run. It sounded like insanity to me.

With nothing to do other than trust them to be civil to each other, I went upstairs and pulled out my favorite blue dress.

Some people in my situation might just leave. They might just let their father figure out how to take care of the saloon on his own.

But I couldn't do that. I couldn't leave him out there like that.

No matter what he had done, he was still my father.

And even though he was selling the saloon off out from under me, for right now, the saloon was still ours.

I was still responsible for it.

So I buttoned up my demurely cut dress, smoothed the long sleeves, then brushed my hair.

I took a moment to wash my face with cool water, washing away the splotch of tears that had streamed down my cheeks.

No matter what happened, I was going to be okay.

I had some things I had to figure out. I had to figure out what it was I was going to do.

My world suddenly felt uncertain and yet at the same time, I sensed a freedom like I had never felt before.

Until now, my life had been laid out in front of me. I would work in the saloon, someday taking it over from my father when he was ready, then I would be the owner of the Whiskey Springs Saloon.

I would live out my life in Whiskey Springs.

On impulse, I wove a blue silk ribbon through my hair, leaving it to fall down my back with my long hair that I left loose.

A lot of things had happened this week. Life changing things.

The most significant, of course, was my father getting shot. That wasn't supposed to happen. The saloon had always been a safe place for us.

Then I had met Shawn. Shawn had opened my eyes to possibilities. Possibilities that did not involve Whiskey Springs. He had me thinking about what it might be like to visit other places. To not be tied down to just one place for the rest of my life.

Then on top of all that, I had discovered that my father had been selling off our family's legacy—the saloon. I didn't even know how long he'd been up to that. He'd been selling off the saloon behind my back and planning on moving back east to be with my mother.

For my father, going east was "moving back." For me, going east was uprooting everything I had ever known and moving somewhere foreign.

I'd been born and bred in Whiskey Springs. The idea of going east to live was so strange to me I couldn't wrap my head around it. Even knowing that my mother was in Savannah didn't help. It didn't help knowing that she had lived there for years and probably, according to my father, wasn't coming back.

I had to admire my father for going to her.

He made excuses about the saloon not doing well, but I knew the saloon was doing just fine. We had no debts and we didn't want for anything.

The truth was he wanted to sell so he could go to be with his wife. I wondered why it had taken him so long.

Deciding to change my shoes while I was at it, I sat down and laced up my second pair of boots.

Feeling sufficiently refreshed, I blew out the candle and headed downstairs.

Somehow I'd thought I would always live here. In this cabin. It had always been my home.

A different way of life was something so outside my way of thinking it had never even occurred to me.

Until now.

Maybe I didn't have to live here forever.

Maybe I could do what Shawn did. Maybe I could travel.

As soon as the thought occurred to me, I chased it away. It wasn't feasible for a woman alone to travel. I could travel to Denver or I could travel to Savannah to visit my mother, sure, but a traveling lifestyle wasn't something a woman, even in this modern world could consider.

Unless I wasn't traveling alone.

When I heard Papa and Shawn laughing, my heart lightened more than it had for a very long time.

"Take care of my girl," I heard Papa say just as I stepped into the parlor.

"Don't worry, Sir," Shawn said, then turned to me. "You ready? If we hurry, we still have some light to walk by."

"What was that about?" I asked as we walked down the front porch steps.

"Nothing," he said, taking my hand. "Your father doesn't want you walking outside at night."

"I see."

It was common knowledge that it wasn't safe to walk alone at night. Somehow I didn't think that was the true extent of what they'd been talking about, but walking along in the waning light of dusk, with my hand in Shawn's, it really didn't seem to matter so much.

Chapter Twenty-Eight

SHAWN

The saloon was busy that night as usual.

I quickly gave up on trying to get any writing done.

I would have to make up my writing work tomorrow. I wasn't worried about it. I always managed to get done what needed to be done and get my manuscripts mailed off on Friday.

Amanda was all over the place. Sometimes she helped me out behind the bar. Sometimes she helped Curtis out in the kitchen. And sometimes she helped serve.

Most of all, she was the one who made sure everything ran smoothly.

When a customer had a problem, she was the one called to resolve it. She made customers happy.

I could see why it had hurt her so much to discover that her father had been selling off the saloon.

It was for all intents and purposes, her saloon. She knew it inside and out.

Customers loved her and she knew them personally. She asked about their children by name. If she didn't know them, she got their names and she remembered them.

Amanda was an incredible woman.

She didn't even seem to know it. Running the saloon was quite simply what she did.

"Can I get two whiskeys?" she asked, coming up to the bar.

"Of course," I said. "When do you take a break?"

"What time is it?"

"Ten fifteen."

"In about two hours," she said as she took the whiskey glasses I set on the bar and took off with them.

I watched her walk toward one of the tables near the piano. Noted the contrast between the scantily clad piano player with her low cut ruffled dress, unabashedly display of ankles and Amanda's demurely cut dress. I was so taken with Amanda that the piano player—I think her name was Missy, maybe, didn't catch my interest in the least.

So in other words, back to Amanda's response, she would take a break after the saloon closed for the night.

I made my way down the bar, refilling glasses.

Tomorrow I would go see Harold Pembroke. I might be overstepping my bounds, but I had some things I wanted to discuss with him.

At Midnight, I closed down the bar, sending everyone home or upstairs to their rooms.

It was half past Midnight before Amanda slowed down enough for me to catch her.

"Don't leave," I told her. "I'm walking you home."

"Okay," she said with a little smile.

I could see the fatigue in her eyes.

She was working too hard.

I had the distinct inclination to take her away from here. There was no reason for her to be working this hard. Life was passing her by while she did nothing more than work.

I closed up the bar, locked away the money, and put on my coat. Ready to go, I went to stand at the door to the kitchen where I could watch for Amanda.

It was almost one o'clock when she finally took off her apron, blew out a breath, and looked around to where her cloak normally hung from one of the pegs near the back door.

Not seeing it, she looked around.

I held up my arm, her cloak draped over it.

We met halfway across the room.

"May I?" I asked, holding her cloak up for her to slip into.

"Thank you," she said, pulling her long hair out of the cloak and letting it fall down her back. "You didn't have to wait for me."

"And how, exactly, would you get home?"

She just shrugged.

"It seemed busier tonight than usual," she said.

"It was busier than usual."

I opened the back door and we stepped outside. The days may

be warm now with spring, but the nights still wore the temperature of winter.

The soft glow of moonlight spilled over us as we headed toward the path leading to her cabin.

I took her hand as we entered the darkness created by thick tree branches overhead.

"Your father told me he's going in to the saloon tomorrow," I said.

"For what?" she asked, her brow furrowed.

"To work. He's ready to be useful again."

"It's too soon." She said the words matter-of-factly.

I held up my free hand. "Don't shoot the messenger. But if I had to bet, no one's going to stop him."

She made a face and shook her head.

"He can be very stubborn."

"I think the stubbornness might be part of why he's been so successful."

"It's no excuse," she said.

I smiled. "I think perhaps you have a bit of his stubbornness in you."

"I'm not stubborn," she said.

"Okay. So anyway. Since your father is going back to work tomorrow, I need to ride into Denver."

"Denver?"

"I have some business I need to take care of."

"Oh. Okay."

We walked in silence the rest of the way to her cabin, then stepped up on the porch.

"Sit with me a few minutes?" I asked, pulling her toward the swing at the end of the porch. "I need to ask you about something."

"It's late," she said. "And you have an early day tomorrow."

"I won't leave until around lunch."

"It's a long ride."

I held the swing while she sat on one end.

"Forward," I said.

"What's that?" she asked, moving her skirts aside so that I could sit next to her.

"Nothing. I was just adding forward to my list of your traits."

"You're keeping a list?" she asked with a look of alarm.

"It helps me when I'm making up characters."

"Then it's a good thing I'm not one of your characters."

An owl in a tree near the porch starting hooting.

She shivered just a little.

"Right?" she asked.

"I'm sorry. What?"

"I'm not one of your characters."

"Right." I sat, leaning back and stretching out my legs.

"You're not very convincing, Shawn Richard."

I grinned.

"There's something you don't know about writers."

"I'm sure there's a lot I don't know," she said, crossly.

"Writers use everything and everyone they encounter in their writing."

"Very well," she said. "What did you want to ask me about?"

"I wanted to know if you'd had time to process everything. With your father and Mr. Pembroke and the saloon."

"Not really," she said.

"But some?" I gently rocked the swing using my feet.

"A little. But not enough to figure anything out."

"It's okay. I'm here if you need to talk."

"You're leaving tomorrow." The crossness in her voice was back.

"But I'll be back," I said. "I promise. Come. Let's get you inside."

After standing up, I held out my hands to help her up.

It would have been so easy, so natural to pull her against me and wrap my arms around her.

But Amanda was a lady and a lady had to be treated with utmost respect.

Born and bred in the south, I knew these things and I lived by them. Amanda was not someone I was going to start breaking my own rules with.

So when we reached the door I kissed her gently on the forehead.

"Be safe, Little One," I said, looking into her deep, fathomless green eyes. "I'll see you soon. I promise."

I didn't make promises lightly.

Chapter Twenty-Nine

Amanda
Three Days Later

IT WAS good to have Papa back in the saloon even if I was still vexed with him.

He spent a lot of time in his office, but also worked behind the bar. Granted, he worked slowly, mostly sitting down. I literally ran circles around him as I took up the slack.

Tonight, a Sunday, was one of those calm nights that happened on occasion. Some claimed it was quiet because it was Sunday, but our regular clientele didn't normally concern themselves with what day of the week it was.

Besides, we had people who came in for the fried chicken and apple pie. It just so happened that some of them wanted a whiskey with their meal.

And while they were there, they stayed to listen to Missy play the piano.

That's how Papa framed it, anyway, to any who might ask and there were some. They were the ones who came with the church and the minister.

But everyone liked Papa and it was hard to judge a man who didn't judge others, especially a man who merely tried to keep the community happy.

It helped that he provided lunch once a month for a church picnic.

I didn't even try to figure out how he could do things like that while he was saying the saloon was struggling to stay afloat financially.

Whenever I thought about it, it brought me back around to the truth. He was selling the saloon so he could move back east to be with Mama.

It was during one of those lulls when Papa summoned me behind the bar to sit next to him.

"You're working too hard," he said. "Sit with me for a few minutes."

"Someone has to do it," I said, but I sat down next to him anyway. The truth was, as long as I stayed busy I didn't have the time to think about how long Shawn had been gone. He'd said he would be gone a day. So I figured two. A trip to Denver and back took two days even for a man just on horseback, no wagon.

But this was the end of day three and he wasn't back yet.

He'd taken everything with him. All his clothes and his

writing materials. I knew because the woman who did the cleaning told Papa and Papa rented the room to someone else.

I bit my tongue and didn't tell him just how wrong that was. That Shawn was coming back.

The truth was I didn't know for sure that he would be coming back.

A man who took all his belongings with him, I knew, had other ideas.

He promised.

"How are you Papa?" I asked.

"Glad to be back at work."

"It's too soon."

"It's never too soon. Anyway. I wanted to talk to you about something."

"What's that?" Those were words I didn't want to hear. Talking was never good news.

"I won't mince words. Mr. Pembroke made his last payment today."

"Excuse me? I think I misunderstood what you said."

"You didn't misunderstand," Papa said. "As of tomorrow, the saloon belongs to Harold Pembroke."

I felt so many emotions that I quite simply went numb.

"It's done then." The words came out flat born of that numbness.

"Yes. It's done."

"Why didn't you tell me?"

"Because I didn't know until today. He was supposed to wait. We were supposed to have another six months before he made the final payment. But he brought a bank draft with all of it. Today."

I looked away. My gaze passed over Missy sitting at the piano. At the group of men playing a game of cards, cigar smoke swirling over their heads. Past the stairs leading up to the second floor where the hotel rooms were.

Finally, my gaze landed on the large picture window with the perfect view of the mountains. The setting sun splashed a rainbow of color across the sky. Just as it did at the end of every day.

Just as it would at the end of every day whether we were here or not.

Papa was talking, but I wasn't listening. Finally, something penetrated the edge of my thoughts and I turned my attention back to him.

"I'm sorry. I wasn't listening. Would you say that again?"

"I said we're leaving for Savannah in two days."

My mouth dropped open and I forced myself to close it.

"Two days. No. We can't. We have the house."

Papa took a deep breath. "I'm afraid we don't."

"What are you saying?" Dread was bringing emotion back to the edge, but I fought it back.

"I sold him the house, too."

"Papa. Please tell me you jest."

"I don't. We're going east. We have no use for it."

"You didn't ask me." I heard my own voice breaking on the words.

Papa put a hand over mine.

"It wasn't your decision Amanda."

"Well." I stood up and straightened to my full height. "I'm not going."

"You have no choice. No place to stay. I might could convince Mr. Pembroke to marry you, but I can't guarantee it."

"No. I will not. Marry. That man." I said the words through clenched teeth. I wanted my father to understand that marrying Mr. Pembroke was not an option.

"Understood," Papa said. "We'll be on the ten o'clock stagecoach Wednesday morning."

Turning, I walked away from him. I walked blindly into the kitchen and out the back door.

I heard Curtis call after me, but I ignored him. Instead, I gathered up my skirts and started running. I ran until I reached the edge of the river.

Leaning against a tree to steady myself, I knew that this time Shawn wasn't here to rescue me from myself.

I had to accept the fact that he wasn't coming back.

And with him not coming back and Papa leaving on the stagecoach, I truly had no reason to stay here.

With tear filled eyes, I looked across the river toward the tall rugged mountains.

My home. But not my home any longer.

I'd loved it here.

It didn't matter.

Fate had other ideas.

My path had taken a turn and I knew I had no choice but to follow it.

Chapter Thirty

AMANDA

When the stagecoach pulled out of Whiskey Springs on Wednesday morning, Papa and I were the only ones on it. Our trunks were secured to the roof. Somehow we had managed to fit all our personal belongings in four trunks. The only exception was the grandfather clock.

Papa had arranged to have the clock shipped east by special courier. Apparently it was one of Mama's heirlooms, handed down through generations on her side of the family.

It was a beautiful day. Warm. The warmest we'd had this year.

The skies were blue with nature providing white wispy clouds for contrast.

As we sat inside the coach, waiting for ten o'clock, I stared out at the saloon. Smoke drifted from the chimneys, just like it always did.

I had cried myself to sleep last night, leaving no tears for today. I had promised myself that I wouldn't take the sadness with me.

Instead I would take determination and some of that stubbornness Shawn had seemed to think I possessed. I disagreed, though, that I was like my father. If I had been in his shoes, I would have asked me if I wanted to sell and to move.

But, it seemed, all Papa could think about was seeing Mama again. He was decidedly chipper this morning. More so than I could ever remember seeing him.

His chipperness was in stark contrast to my surliness. Surliness, I had conceded, was different from tears.

So I brought surliness along with my determination.

"Everything will be okay," Papa said.

Nodding, I sent him a quick, forced smile, before turning my gaze back to the saloon.

It didn't matter that I had been thinking about leaving here before any of this happened. If I'd had some choice in the matter, I might feel differently about it. I might not.

The coach rocked as the driver boarded.

It looked like there would be no other passengers, at least not yet. There would be plenty of opportunity to pick up others along the way.

As the coach began to move, the wheels crunching on the soft dirt, I swallowed the queasiness that I felt.

I would make the most of it.

Later on, I would worry about leaving behind the saloon and

cabin that I thought would one day be mine. The saloon and cabin where I had grown up.

But right now, the thing that hurt me even worse was not getting to see Shawn again.

I worried that something had happened to him. Then right behind that, I'd be mad at him for breaking his promise to return. It was a vicious cycle in my head.

As it was, there was no way I would ever know one way or the other. Not now.

It was better this way, I told myself.

It was better than watching the door, waiting for him to return.

This was definitely better.

Someday, perhaps, it might even possibly feel better.

Perhaps. Perhaps not.

We headed down the curving mountain road toward Denver. I settled into my warm cloak with the soft fur lining and closed my eyes.

If I closed my eyes and pretended to sleep, my father wouldn't try to talk to me.

I didn't want his chipperness disturbing my surliness.

Chapter Thirty-One

SHAWN

My business in Denver took longer than I had expected. Certainly longer than I had planned.

I'd been so eager to return to Whiskey Springs that I had left Denver much too late in the day. Unfortunately, there was no moonlight tonight so I was forced to stop and make camp.

It had been awhile since I had misjudged my distance between towns enough to have to sleep on the ground.

Good thing I carried a bedroll with me for just such occurrences. If I'd known I was going to be using it, I would have had it laundered before I left Denver. Still. It was better than sleeping on the ground or trying to navigate the rocky mountain trails in the darkness. The last thing I needed was for me and my horse to end up at the bottom of a ravine.

After I got a little fire going, I dragged a fallen log over and used it for a bench.

I stretched my hands out toward the fire as the biscuits I'd had the foresight to bring with me heated on an iron skewer.

It might be approaching summer, but winter was still on night duty.

It was Wednesday night. I'd been gone from Whiskey Springs for almost a week. I'd used my unexpected delay, at least, to finish up my book for the week, so I had that going for me.

That meant that I could focus on Amanda for the rest of the week.

"You were gone too long."

I jumped, nearly falling off the log.

Ophelia sat next to me on the other end of the log, wearing her usual white gauzy dress.

"What the he—?"

"Hello Shawn," she said, interrupting my outburst of profanity.

"What are you doing out here? Aren't you supposed to be at the saloon?"

She shrugged. "You'd think with you being a writer and all, you'd know a little more about ghosts."

"Not my genre," I said under my breath.

"Well. Ghosts are unconfined by place and time."

"Good to know. But why are you here?"

Ophelia raised her chin as though she was offended by my question.

Were ghosts so easily offended then? Perhaps her being a female explained it more than her being a ghost.

"I thought you might need my assistance."

"Okay," I said. "If you think it, then I probably do. Why did you say I was gone too long?"

"Well," Ophelia said, her feathers smoothed. "A lot happened in Whiskey Springs while you were gone."

"I'm on my way back there now. I was unavoidably detained."

"There's no reason for you to go there."

"I'm going to see Amanda."

Ophelia shook her head.

"She isn't there."

"Where is she?"

"You might recall passing a stagecoach a few hours ago."

I tensed. I did indeed recall passing a stagecoach. I'd thought about Amanda when I saw it, but I'd had no reason to think she might be on it.

"She's in Denver then?"

"No. Not exactly." Ophelia primly adjusted her sleeves. "I might have slowed them down a bit."

"Slowed them down how?"

"I dropped a tree across the road. A big one." She seemed quite proud of herself.

"Ghosts can do that?"

"No. Not normally," she said, looking a bit concerned. "I think it might be my last hurrah."

"That sound ominous."

"It's time. I'm pretty sure helping you with Amanda was my last task as a ghost."

I didn't know what to say. I had a lot of questions for her, but they all seemed too personal to ask.

"I should go then," I said. "Find her."

"You should wait until morning. Already it's getting foggy and I don't think it's a good idea for you to be out there on the trail. In the dark."

"That's why I stopped."

"Smart. I don't always know about young people these days."

"You aren't old," I said, carefully pulling my hot biscuit off the skewer. "Want some?"

She gave me a look.

"Right. Sorry."

"What else can you tell me?" I asked.

Ophelia was looking upwards now, no longer focused on me.

When my horse neighed, I glanced over my shoulder.

I held out one of my biscuits for him and he ate it, in one big bite, out of my hand.

When I looked back toward Ophelia, she was gone.

"Well," I said to myself. "I guess that's that."

And tomorrow at daybreak, I'd be heading back toward Denver to find Amanda.

All thanks to Ophelia.

Chapter Thirty-Two

AMANDA

We were what I estimated to be about two hours out of Denver when the stagecoach was delayed by a large, healthy oak tree lying across the road.

Papa and I got out of the coach to join the driver as he studied the tree.

"It looks like a perfectly healthy tree to me," the driver said. "No storm either."

"What do you think caused it?" Papa asked.

"Would have said beavers," the driver said. "but it's not cut. Just pulled right up by the roots."

"How do we move it?" Papa asked, always the practical one.

"Got a saw on you?" the driver asked.

"Do you?"

"Got a hatchet. I'll get to work on it."

"Why don't we just turn around?" I asked, with barely disguised hopefulness. "Go back to Whiskey Springs."

Both men looked at me as though I was daft.

I just shrugged, pulled one of Shawn's books out of my large travel bag, and found a boulder to sit on.

After an hour of the driver working on the tree, it became clear that we weren't going anywhere tonight. Papa couldn't help because he was still recovering from his gunshot wound. The poor driver was sweating profusely and I was beginning to fear for his health.

Yet neither man would admit that I was right about turning around.

As I sat in front of the little fire, I wondered if I should be upset about the delay.

I wasn't.

I had not been ready to leave Whiskey Springs, so I welcomed the delay even if it did mean spending the night in the stagecoach while my father and the driver slept on the ground.

By morning, however, I was rethinking my delight at the delay. The stagecoach was a most uncomfortable place to sleep and I woke stiff to the sound of the stagecoach driver chopping away at the tree again.

I climbed out of the stagecoach, stretched, and joined my father in front of a meager fire.

"Coffee?" he asked.

"How did you? Never mind."

I assumed the stagecoach driver had come prepared with coffee and mugs.

"Sure," I said.

The coffee he handed me in a tin cup tasted bitter and disgusting. When I drank coffee, Curtis always made sure I had warm milk mixed in with it.

No warm milk out here.

"Is he making any progress?" I asked.

"Seems to be. It's a really big tree."

"Very strange, isn't it?" I asked. "Maybe it's a sign we aren't supposed to go."

"Has anyone ever told you that you have a stubborn streak?"

"Actually. Yes," I said, with a little sigh. "Seems to run in the family."

"Huh."

"Someone's coming," I said, hearing hoofbeats coming along the trail toward us.

"Good," Papa said. "Maybe they can help with this tree so we can be on our way."

"Maybe." I stood up. Straightened my skirts. Whoever it was came from the direction of Whiskey Springs.

Not Denver. I was more interested in someone heading this way from Denver.

My heart started pounding loudly in my ears as the horse came closer.

I'll never know just how I recognized him, but I did.

It was Shawn.

I stood frozen, my head not daring to believe what my heart was telling me.

He dismounted and removed his hat before I knew my heart was right.

"Shawn."

Meeting me halfway across the distance, he picked me up by the waist and swung me around in a circle.

"You're here," I said when my feet were back on the ground. "How did you find me?"

"I had a little help." He glanced at the tree. "That's a really big tree."

"Very strange," I said.

"You have no idea."

"What?"

"I need to talk to you." He took my hand. "Can I borrow your daughter, Mr. Gray?"

Not waiting for an answer, Shawn took my hand and led me away toward the sound of the rushing river.

We found a boulder along the bank and I sat down. He sat down for moment, then just stood up again.

"Hi," he said, stopping in front of me.

"Hi."

"I 'um." He removed his hat and set it on the boulder next to me. "My business took longer than I expected."

"My father sold the saloon and our house."

"Already?" he asked. "I thought we had more time."

"We?"

"Yes," he said, sitting down again and taking my hands.

"What do you mean?"

"I have some options for you. I need to know what you want."

"I want..." I squeezed my eyes tightly together then opened them again and looked into his sparkling blue eyes. I couldn't finish the sentence. Not yet.

"I don't have any choices. My father sold the house and he's taking me to Savannah to live with my mother."

"That's one choice. You have others."

I shook my head. "I can't see them."

"I know." He looked over his shoulder. The steady chopping of the axe had stopped.

"You can go with your father," he said.

"You said I had other options."

"We can go back to Whiskey Springs. Get the saloon and the house back."

"How can we do that?"

"I have a bank draft right here." He patted his shirt pocket. "It's an amount that Harold Pembroke and I agreed upon."

"You have the money to buy it back?" I knew I sounded incredulous, but I didn't care. I was.

He smiled and kissed me on the forehead.

"As I mentioned, you have a lot to learn about writers. They pay me quite well to do what I enjoy."

Back to Whiskey Springs? This was not something I had considered. And truth be known, now that it was offered, I wasn't sure it was what I wanted.

"What's the other option?"

"You can come with me. We can travel. We can go wherever you want to go. I can show you places I've been. And we can see new places. We can go to Montana."

"Montana."

"I've always wanted to go to Montana."

"It sounds like a long way away." It also sounded exciting.

But it sounded too good to be true.

"I can't just go to Montana with you. It wouldn't be proper."

He slid off the Boulder, getting on one knee.

"It would be proper for you to go as Mrs. Shawn Richard."

"I 'um. I don't know what to say."

"Say yes."

"I don't think you asked a question," I said, unable to think straight.

"Stubborn," he said, but he was smiling. "Amanda Gray? Will you marry me?"

I hadn't wanted to leave Whiskey Springs, but now I didn't want to go back.

Whiskey Springs had been my home for a time, but now my home was somewhere else.

Now my home was with Shawn.

The winds of fate had changed direction and I had no choice but to go with them.

"Yes." I might be from a small town nestled in the mountains of Colorado, but I knew better than to fight the winds of fate.

Besides, why would I want to?

Epilogue

Amanda

"They call it Big Sky Country," Shawn said.

"I see why."

The Montana sky stretched endlessly. The sky seemed so low, I could almost reach up and touch it. Snow-capped mountains rose in the distance at the far end of the western sky.

It looked like home.

We rode along on the buckboard of a covered wagon, our belongings in the wagon behind us. The roads were bumpier here than any other place we had been. That was saying a lot. We had been a lot of places.

We spent at least a week wherever we went. Shawn wrote a book during the week. Mailed it on Friday. While he wrote, I read. I read everything he wrote.

When he wasn't writing, we explored whatever town we were staying in. We'd visited his sister Ember and her husband, then we had visited his sister Olivia and her husband. Both of them had two children each.

We'd spent our first winter in Denver as we had planned. We'd studied maps and everything we could find to read, which wasn't much.

But in the end, we had decided to make the trip to Montana. We'd bought the covered wagon just to come here.

Life with Shawn so far had been an adventure.

One I wouldn't trade for anything.

He thanked the ghost of Ophelia for it.

I thanked the winds of fate.

No matter what it was that had brought us together, I was thankful.

Not only had I gotten a new, unexpected life, but I had gotten Shawn.

Sometimes when I looked at him, I still couldn't believe that we were married.

"We should be getting close to the little town," he said.

"Good. I'm starving."

"Are you feeling better?"

"Just a little tired."

"But you're happy?"

"Of course," I said with a smile. "Why would you ask me that?"

"Because being married to a writer with no home isn't the kind of thing most ladies would be happy with."

"I'm not like most ladies," I said, just as I had told him a thousand times. "Besides, when the time is right, we'll get a place of our own. Right?"

"That's right," he said.

"There's the Buffalo Inn they told us about." I pointed up ahead. "We can eat now."

"You had lunch," he said. "I hope you're not coming down with something."

I looked at him sideways.

He shrugged. "My mother used to say that whenever a person was getting sick, they would eat more right before."

"I've never heard that. I hope I'm not getting sick."

He stopped the wagon in front of the door and a young lad came out to take our horses.

"Take good care of them," Shawn told him.

"Yes sir. Just go on inside. My ma will have a room for you."

"Montana seems nice already," I said.

Shawn dismounted first, then put his arms around my waist and swung me down.

"Oh," I said, pressing a hand against my stomach.

"Are you okay? Did I hurt you?"

"No. I just felt a little queasy, that's all."

"You're just tired."

He took my hand and led me inside.

"Hello. I'm Mrs. Porter. Come on in. I have a room ready for you."

"We're Shawn and Amanda Richard."

"Welcome to the Buffalo Inn. One of my boys will bring in your trunks."

"Just the one up front," Shawn said. We don't need all of them tonight.

"Let me show you your room, then I'll make you something to eat."

"Thank you so much," I said. "I'm starving."

"That's normal for a young lady in your condition. Come on back to your room."

Confused, I looked at Shawn as we followed her back to our room.

"What do you mean?" I asked. "My condition."

"My dear. When is the last time you saw your mama?" Mrs. Porter looked at me before she opened the door to the guest room.

"Ten years, I guess."

"Oh my. Well. Here's your room."

"Mrs. Porter," I said, placing a hand lightly on her arm. "What condition are you referring to?"

Mrs. Porter glanced over at Shawn who was looking out the window, then leaned over and whispered something in my ear.

"Oh."

"Well. I'll leave you two to freshen up. One of my boys will come get you when supper is ready."

"What did she tell you?" Shawn asked after she'd closed the door behind her. "What condition is she talking about?"

"Shawn," I said, whispering the words as I searched his eyes. "She thinks I'm with child."

"With—" He grinned and swept me up in his arms. "I should have recognized the signs. Being queasy and hungry. I have two sisters but I wasn't around them when they were expecting."

"Are you happy?" I asked.

"I'm ecstatic. We're going to have a baby."

He swept me around and stopped at the window, leaving me a little out of breath.

"Look at that. Montana is beautiful, isn't it?"

"It is beautiful. But—" How could he have just jumped right along to a new topic? A baby was a big, life changing event. It was more than just a brief acknowledgement.

"If you like it here, we can build a cabin. Make a home."

"Oh." So he hadn't just jumped topics. He had a plan.

"Let's take our time," he said. "Find the perfect place."

So overcome with emotion, I was unable to speak, I just nodded.

Wherever Shawn was. That was the perfect place for me.

But we would find it. We would find the perfect place to make our home. We'd start from the ground up. Just like we'd talked about. Something that would be just ours.

A place that just the two of us would build together.

Keep Reading for a preview of
Accidentally Forever...

KATHRYN KALEIGH

Accidentally Forever

THE ASHTONS
FOREVER AND EVER

Accidentally Forever
PREVIEW

Chapter 1
Grace Miller

JUST ONE MORE PATIENT and I could call it a day.

I sat at my desk with my back to the window. On purpose. Too many distractions to try to work facing the window. I usually even lowered the shades when patients were in my office.

This fifth floor office had a clear view of the 610 West Loop looking out toward River Oaks. I couldn't see downtown Houston from here, but if I went up on the roof I could. From here downtown was so far away, it looked like a tiny cluster of buildings. Something a child might have built out of blocks.

No one went on the roof this time of year. Full on August in Houston was not the time for taking a break on the roof even if it had nice seating to enjoy the nice view. The building managers were talking about making the rooftop a green space with orange trees, but so far no one had moved in that direction.

Slipping my heels off, I rested my bare feet on the tops of my shoes. I wore what I considered appropriately conservative work attire. A dark gray pencil skirt with a matching blazer that hit at my waist. A white collared shirt. And of course, my heels.

I dragged the comb out of my hair and let my long hair swirl around my shoulders as I stretched my arms and got the blood flowing.

I had one hour to sit at my desk and catch up on notes for the day. I opened up my laptop and logged into the charting program my business partner insisted we use.

Me? I was okay with notes typed into a Word document and printed out supplemented by my handwritten notes neatly filed in folders and kept in a locked filing cabinet. A system that had served me well for the two years I'd had my own practice.

But going in with Jonathan had been a smart business move. He had more experience which meant he had more patients and not just that. He was on staff with the mental hospital and got frequent referrals. More than he could handle.

That's where I came in. I'd been with Jonathan for three months now and I was steadily building my patient load. At the rate I was going, Jonathan was going to have to bring in another psychologist before long.

He would have to lease another office if he did that and probably hire a receptionist. I had his old office and he had taken an empty larger one down the hall. There wasn't really space for a receptionist, but he would figure it out.

I was already working late at least three nights a week, one of them being tonight. I had to decide if I wanted to add Saturdays or another late night.

The office space was in a recently renovated building with freshly painted walls and hardwood floors. Very clean. Very modern.

I tried to make sure my space wasn't intimidating. I kept a cinnamon and vanilla candle lit and fresh flowers, currently white daisies, on the corner of my desk. I personally preferred the scent of daffodils, but the florist had been out when I'd stopped by this morning. Daisies were fine though.

This side of the office was what I considered the working side. Desk and a small bookcase with books I used often including the DSM.

The other side of the office was the therapeutic side. Two comfortable chairs and a love seat. One of the chairs was mine. I let the patients choose whether they wanted to sit on the sofa or the other chair.

No coffee table between us. Just a big bookcase with books that were more likely to appeal to patients. Self-help books, mostly. A strong believer in bibliotherapy, I kept it well stocked with my favorite books that I tended to give away.

All part of the cost of doing business.

I was fairly fast at charting, so I was well into my last patient's notes when my phone alarm went off, reminding me to get ready for my seven o'clock patient.

All I knew about him was that he was a twenty-seven-year-old male. I usually had a diagnosis when they were referrals from the hospital, but this man had self-referred through our website.

I saved everything on the computer, logged out, and got ready for my patient. A cold bottle of water on the end table for the client. A new client intake form for me. It was just a habit to have it with me. I never looked at the intake sheets anymore. I had all the questions memorized and I was good at remembering what we talked about.

When the elevator opened, I glanced at the clock on the wall. My patient was five minutes early. I took this as a good sign.

Since people tended to get turned around coming off the elevator, I went to the door.

This man, however, was walking right toward my office.

Maybe walking wasn't quite the right word. Sauntering was a more accurate word.

Tall and lean, he was handsome with a sexy five-o'clock shadow that many men would envy.

As he sauntered toward me, pulling off aviator sunglasses as he walked, he struck a feminine chord deep down in my reptilian brain. I recognized the way my heart rate sped up and butterflies took flight in my stomach.

He's a patient.

I tamped down those primitive feelings of attraction and gave him my most professional smile.

In the process of tamping down my attraction, I felt myself leaning toward the other end of the spectrum. Extremely professional.

"Come in," I said. "Have a seat."

Accidentally Forever
PREVIEW

Chapter 2
Benjamin Ashton

I VALETED my rental car at my buddy Jonathan's office building and headed straight for the fifth floor.

I could have taken an Uber from the airport, but sometimes I just liked the challenge of navigating city traffic on a busy freeway.

Since I had been here when Jonathan moved into this office building, I was more than familiar with the layout.

The spacious lobby with tall ceilings and bright chandeliers would be intimidating to a lot of people, but Jonathan—Dr. Jonathan Baker—didn't worry about such things. He was going for the high-end clients and did so unabashedly. Ambition was his middle name and from what I could tell, he was doing quite well in that direction.

The building had tall imposing live green plants placed strategically around as well as oversized furniture where people could wait for their appointments or just sit and use the WIFI.

The building held all sorts of professional offices. It had a psychiatrist, a chiropractor, a whole floor for attorneys, and a floor for some kind of stock trading.

The rent in this place alone required a certain level of clients. Apparently Jonathan knew what he was doing. The last time I talked to him—about six months ago, maybe longer—he'd been talking about expanding his business. Hiring on some help.

Not a bad idea, but I recommended he put an attorney on retainer.

Not only did I come from a family of entrepreneurs located in Pittsburgh, but I worked for Noah Worthington of Skye Travels. Skye Travels was the premier private airline company in the country.

Noah had taken one small airplane and built a billion dollar company on his own. He was a legend in the field of aviation. New graduates lined up at his door to be interviewed. I was no exception.

I'd been lucky. He'd branched out to Pittsburgh, and was looking to hire a pilot for there.

Long story, but it was around that same time that I learned that Noah Worthington was actually my grandfather's brother.

So he was Uncle Noah. An odd turn of events that had turned out well. The two brothers had gotten reacquainted after having lost touch with each other for most of their adult lives.

It was hard to think of him as Uncle Noah. Instead, I mostly thought of him as the boss.

At any rate, I knew a little bit about starting and running a business.

The elevator that took me up to the fifth floor had that fresh clean scent that smelled like success.

I should have called him. He often worked late, doing paperwork, but it was possible he had a client at this late hour. It was okay. I didn't mind waiting.

I stepped off the elevator into a wide carpeted hallway and headed straight for his office. Realizing I still wore my sun glasses, I pulled them off and blinked as my eyes adjusted.

I nearly came to a stop and would have except that my feet had unstoppable momentum.

A young lady stood at Jonathan's door. Maybe he'd hired some help already.

"Come on in," she said. "Have a seat."

Not one to argue with a pretty girl, I did as she asked.

She was a petite thing, even in high heels, dressed in a professional skirt and blazer.

Professional down to the white collared shirt.

I followed her inside the office. I recognized the view and although the office had the same general arrangement, things looked different.

The couch was new. One of the chairs. White daisies on a vase on the desk. A candle throwing out a mixture of vanilla and cinnamon scent.

Definitely different from Jonathan's décor.

I decided to try out the couch.

She sat across from me, leaning forward, holding a clipboard on her lap.

"I'm pleased that you came in," she said.

"Me too."

"I'd like to start with some basic questions. Then we can see if we're a good match and set up a plan of treatment."

A good match, huh? That was one part I was feeling confident about. As far as a plan of treatment, that sounded a little out of my league.

I glanced over my shoulder.

"I was expecting Jonathan to be here."

"He and I work together," she said. He's just down the hall. Since he's booked ahead several weeks, I was hoping you would give me a chance to work with you."

I realized right then that I was at one of those crossroads that could be life-altering.

The sensation was a little like flying an airplane. I made decisions every day that I hoped led to the best outcome. I had learned to go with my instinct and not second-guess myself. It had served me well so far.

"Okay," I said, giving her a little smile.

"I should introduce myself. I'm Dr. Grace Miller."

I was headed down that slippery slope and although there was still time to jump off, I was intrigued enough to play along.

"Benjamin Ashton."

A brief flash of confusion flashed across her face, but was quickly gone. She didn't recognize my name.

"I don't know much about you," she said. "Your application answers didn't go much further than you being twenty-seven."

"I like my privacy," I said.

Since I was playing along, I decided to be as truthful as I could.

"I understand. So do I. I have just some basic questions to get out of the way. Questions that will help me get to know you better."

"Go ahead," I leaned back, getting comfortable, and stretched one arm out across the back of the couch.

I'd been on a lot of dates. Usually getting to know each other was a little more subtle. Maybe this was a better, more straightforward way to get acquainted.

"Let's start with your occupation."

"I'm a pilot," I said.

"I see. A commercial pilot?"

"I work for a private airline company based here in town."

"Skye Travels?" she asked.

"Is there any other?" I asked with a smile.

"Not that I'm aware of. Do you have any siblings?"

She hadn't so much as glanced at the clipboard in her lap.

"I have two older sisters, one older brother, and one younger brother."

"You have a really big family. What was that like for you? Growing up?"

"I had a good childhood. Our parents were strict, but fair."

"You were close to your siblings?"

"Mostly my younger brother, but we were all close."

"What about now?"

"Now?" I ran a hand along my chin. "Now they're all married."

"And you? Are you married?"

"I'm single."

She didn't even miss a beat. Talking to her reminded me in some ways of having a conversation with Jonathan. He was persistent also. Persistent and straightforward.

"What's it like being the only single person in your family?"

"They're all happy."

She leaned forward, looking into my eyes. Her eyes were a lovely shade of green. The color of a meadow seen from ten thousand feet in the bright sunshine of spring.

Her red bow shaped lips parted slightly, curved into a little smile that she seemed to be fighting a losing battle with. I could tell she was trying, rather unsuccessfully, not to smile.

"But what about you? What's it like for you?"

I shrugged.

"I now have two more sisters and two more brothers."

"You're close to your in-laws."

"We're all close. We all spend a lot of time together."

I opened my mouth to tell her that we all lived in the same house, but closed it. It wasn't something I told people quite simply because it was one of those things that was hard for people to understand.

It was hard for people to understand that our house was large enough to comfortably hold six families. Most people didn't even call it a house. They called it a manor—which it was.

I also didn't tell people that we had a cook, a gardener, and a housekeeper and all of them lived on the grounds.

Those were things I kept to myself.

"Tell me about your parents."

"They worked a lot, still do, but they always had time for us."

"They were supportive of your decision to become a pilot?"

I looked blankly at her a moment, then cleared my throat.

That was the other thing I didn't tell people. Not only did my uncle own the airline, but both of my brothers and both of my brothers-in-law were pilots.

"Yes," I said. "They are very supportive."

I was finding this conversation difficult. It was hard talking to her without telling her everything.

And even though there were things I didn't go around telling people, I wanted to tell her everything.

Accidentally Forever
PREVIEW

Chapter 3
Grace

WITH THE CITY ambiance that even drawn shades couldn't block out, I studied my new client.

I wanted to go back to my computer. I was decent at remembering names. I'd had it in my head that his name was Bradford... something. Not Benjamin. Maybe I'd read it wrong. But no. I distinctly remembered making a folder in the computer program with the name Bradford... something.

I'd straighten that out later. Couldn't very well jump up in the middle of a session to go to my computer because I was confused on his name.

So far I didn't see anything that would guide me toward a

diagnosis. Jonathan would probably say he was enmeshed with his family, but I believed that to be a good thing. Families these days were too scattered and family support was one of those fundamental things that, in my experience, everyone needed.

When patients had family support, unless those families were completely dysfunctional, they typically fared much better than those who didn't have family support.

I had enough history from him for now. It was time to get some more pertinent information.

"Have you ever been hospitalized for mental health reasons?"

"No," he said.

"Have you ever had any kind of counseling?"

"No."

"You didn't indicate on your contact information anything that you might want to work on. Is there anything in particular that you'd like to talk about?"

He didn't answer right away. I gave him time to think. It was one of those thirty second pauses that seemed to last forever.

"It's just nice to have someone who listens."

If there was anything diagnosable about him, it was going to take some time to get him to talk about it. Private people were usually like that.

"It's hard for you to trust people," I said.

"I don't know if I'd go that far."

"But you don't have anyone you're comfortable talking to."

"I have a good friend. I talk to him."

"Yeah? When is the last time you spoke to him?"

"Christmas, I think. Maybe New Year's."

"So it's been about six months?"

"I guess so."

I wasn't concerned with that. It was typical guy behavior. Guys could go years without talking and still consider themselves good friends. When they picked up the phone, they just picked up the conversation like they had spoken last week.

It wasn't usually like that for women. I didn't like to generalize, but I saw it all the time. In order for girlfriends to remain girlfriends, they had to keep up with each other on a regular basis. Weekly. Sometimes even daily.

I had one friend, but he was a guy—also a graduate student.

Graduate school, then working didn't allow a lot of time for hanging out with friends.

The only people I'd gone out with socially during graduate school was fellow graduate students and all we talked about was psychology.

So I was in no place to judge Benjamin for going six months without talking to his best friend.

"What kinds of things do you do for fun?"

"I fly airplanes."

He said it without hesitation.

"I mean outside of your job."

"Occasional family time. A movie here and there. Grilling outside on family days."

"So no hobbies?"

"Flying is my hobby and my career."

"It's who you are."

"Yes." He sounded surprised that I understood that.

I knew what it was like to eat, sleep, and breathe one's career. It was what it took.

Having a career like psychology or aviation took complete focus.

My watch vibrated, telling me that we only had ten minutes left in the session.

"We only have about ten minutes left," I said. "So I'd like to go over what we talked about."

"Okay. Sure." He leaned forward and looked into my eyes. His eyes were a lovely deep cerulean blue that a girl could fall into.

How was it that a guy like this was still single?

Maybe that was something he wanted to work on.

"You're a pilot for Skye Travels. Flying is your passion. The one thing that's a constant in your life.

"You're close to your family. Two brothers, one older, one younger, and two older sisters. They're all married and you like their spouses. Am I right so far?"

"Impressively so."

"You have good family support and a good friend that you can talk to about just about anything. You're here because you just want someone to talk to."

"Yes," he said.

"Does this time and day work for you?"

He looked away for a moment. Gave me another one of those thirty second forever silences.

"I have an erratic schedule. I never know where I'll be."

"I can see where having someone to talk to could be a problem. Why don't you use the scheduling feature on the website to schedule your next session yourself. I'll recognize your name and I'll know you aren't a new client. Does that sound good to you?"

"It sounds okay to me," he said.

"So. Our time is up for now. Is there anything you'd like to add before you go?"

Clients invariably saved their true reason for coming to therapy for the last five minutes of the session. I always braced myself when I asked that question. I knew of psychologists had stopped asking for that very reason.

"Nothing to add," he said. "I enjoyed talking to you."

"Likewise."

He stood up from the couch and I stood up with him, holding my clipboard with both hands at my waist.

"Until next week then," he said.

"Next week. Whenever works for you."

"I'll let you know when I'm back in town."

"Take care, Benjamin," I said, walked to the door, and opened it.

"Good night," he said.

After stepping out into the hallway, I went back to my computer. I wanted to double-check his name. It wasn't like me to get the name of a new client wrong.

I went straight to the computer and logged in.

Ah ha. I had been right.

My client's name was Bradford.

And Bradford had sent an email asking to reschedule.

Accidentally Forever
PREVIEW

Chapter 4
Benjamin

I CHECKED my watch as I stepped out of Dr. Miller's office.

I'd been in her office for fifty minutes, but it didn't seem like it. It seemed like I'd been there for about fifteen minutes. Time had flown by.

I stood in the hallway and considered. Jonathan had obviously moved his office. And he had obviously added someone into his fold. Just as he had said he would.

The problem at the moment was that I didn't know where to find Jonathan.

I walked to the end of the hall, checking names on doors as I went.

And there at the end of the hallway, I found his name on the door.

Dr. Jonathan Baker.

Since his door was closed, I sent him a text.

> Hey. I'm outside your new office.

He wouldn't answer if he was with a patient.

But he answered right back.

> JONATHAN
>
> I'm at the bar downstairs.

This day was just getting stranger and stranger.

> Do you want company?

> JONATHAN
>
> Sure. Come down.

Going back the way I came, I passed by Dr. Grace Miller's closed office. I was still a little dazed by that whole experience.

I had just gone through an entire counseling session.

I stopped, my hand almost to the elevator button.

Well hell.

I had just taken up an hour of her time that had been reserved for someone else.

That hardly seemed right.

I had to pay her for her time. For me the hour had been a casual interesting interlude, but for her, it had been work.

I never carried cash anymore, but I did keep one check on me for emergencies. I still, in this modern day and age, occasionally encountered someone who did not take credit cards, but oddly enough, would take a check.

Tugging the folded check out of my wallet, I wrote it out to her, leaving the amount blank, and signed it.

I wrote a note on the back.

I know I wasn't your scheduled client. Please fill in your rate for new clients.

I hesitated. I was running out of room, but I had so much I wanted to say. I boiled it down to the gist of it all.

Thank you for listening.

Feeling much better, I slid the check underneath her door and went straight to the elevator.

Maybe I'd have just one beer with Jonathan. It was early and I didn't have another flight until in the morning.

I needed to figure out just how much I was going to tell him about my hour with Dr. Miller.

Nothing. That's what I was going to tell him.

He'd probably tell me it was unethical pretending to be a client when I wasn't.

It wouldn't matter, or maybe it would make matters even worse, that I had enjoyed talking to Grace.

I got off the elevator, went outside, and walked across the street to the little bar where he and I had spent quite a few hours in our younger days. These days it wasn't like Jonathan to be here. He was typically home with his wife if he wasn't working.

But then again, as I had admitted to Grace, it had been six months since I had spoken to him. I had no way of knowing what was going on in his life right now.

He and I needed to do a better job of keeping up with each other.

I stepped into the upscale bar called simply *Equinox* and looked around for Jonathan.

The bar, a favorite hangout for the after work crowd was loud and the servers were hopping.

Jonathan, seeing me walk in, held up a hand and I spotted him across the room.

I slid into the booth across from him.

"What are you doing here?" I asked. "Why aren't you with Victoria?"

"Victoria left me."

Keep Reading
Accidentally Forever...

Kathryn Kaleigh writes sweet contemporary romance, time travel romance, and historical romance.

kathrynkaleigh.com

Milton Keynes UK
Ingram Content Group UK Ltd.
UKHW021938201124
451474UK00014B/1115

9 798330 485598